"If you care so little for your reputation and mine," he said in a harsh whisper, "I might as well share the bounty, too." He pulled her closer, until her body was pressed against his hard chest, and then he lowered his lips to hers.

Rosellen was staggered by the weight of his anger, the accusations, the fact that he was actually kissing her. This might even be worth getting ruined over. She kissed him back, with all her inexperienced but awakening passion, just to make certain.

She was certain. And Rosellen was equally sure the viscount was kissing her only out of anger that she'd caused him more annoyance. He didn't like her, didn't respect her, and never believed a word she said, the worm. So she hauled back her broken wrist and cracked him along the jaw with her new plaster cast. . . .

MISS LOCKHARTE'S LETTERS

Barbara Metzger

FAWCETT CREST • NEW YORK

A Fawcett Crest Book
Published by The Ballantine Publishing Group
Copyright © 1998 by Barbara Metzger

http://www.randomhouse.com

Library of Congress Catalog Card Number: 97-94535

ISBN 0-449-00170-9

Manufactured in the United States of America

First Edition: June 1998

10 9 8 7 6 5 4 3 2 1

This one's for Jimmie,
for taking the dog's temperature,
for sucking the water out of the headlamp,
and for being there, my friend

Chapter One

$\mathcal{M}$iss Rosellen Lockharte was dying. She could live with that, in a manner of speaking, if not for the noise and the lights. Why couldn't she be permitted to shuffle off this mortal coil in peace? Then again, when had she ever had any peace? Certainly not since coming to Miss Merrihew's Select Academy for Young Females of Distinction. Young Females of Disease and Contagion, more likely, Rosellen considered as she huddled miserably on her bed, dying of the influenza epidemic that had struck the girls' school. It wasn't even her own bed. No one could be spared to tend to the most junior and least-favored instructor at Miss Merrihew's in her tiny attic room under the rafters, of course. Therefore, Rosellen and her belongings had been hauled and harried down three flights of stairs to the dormitory room that had been turned into an infirmary, where she could be equally as ignored and uncared for. Now she was separated from the other sick females and their moans, groans, weeping, and retching by a rickety screen. Nothing separated her aching eyes from the lamps left constantly burning except for a sodden towel over her forehead, when one of the maids could remember to bring her a cloth or a bowl of water. A cup of tea or some broth seemed beyond the resources of the overworked staff or past the scope of Miss Merrihew's munificence toward her least profitable investment. Providentially, since Miss Lockharte's stomach would have rebelled at the sight of food anyway, there was none at her bedside. Why waste a stale muffin on a poorly paid, poorly appreciated penmanship teacher? She would be as hard and dry as that missing muffin soon enough. Worm toast, that's what Rosellen would be. A sob escaped her parched, cracked lips.

"Here now, miss," she heard from nearby, along with the clatter of a tray, which meant it was time for medicine. That would be the overworked maid, Fanny, for none of the teaching staff came near the infirmary, fearing contagion. "No call for carryin' on that way. The doctor says you should be done with your misery by tomorrow."

"I know," Rosellen whimpered. "I heard him."

The local physician had stood right by the old screen—she'd heard its unsteady legs scraping the floor—and said, "I'm sorry to say, but there's no hope for this one, Miss Merrihew. She'll be gone by morning, I fear." He hadn't even bothered to whisper, thinking her already unconscious, Rosellen supposed.

She choked back another sob. "It isn't fair."

"You can say that again, miss. Lucy's gone off to her mum's an' Aggie says she's comin' down with the ague, so there's only me to do all the fetchin' and carryin'. You'd think the mistress would hire on extra staff for all the extra work, but not that one. Part with an extra groat? I should live to see the day."

So should Rosellen, if miracles still happened, but that wasn't what she'd meant. Life was unfair. Of course it was, everyone knew that. But this, this debacle of dying before one's twenty-first birthday, seemed a particularly nasty twist of fate. Rosellen Lockharte was going to die before she'd ever lived. She'd never danced the waltz, never seen fireworks, never even had a dog of her own. Now she'd never have a child of her own, a garden, a lover. She had nothing to show for her twenty years either, nothing to hold up as a recommendation of her worth except for the fancy *p*'s and *q*'s of the pampered daughters of polite society. Heaven knew, and surely St. Peter would, too, that those same decorative darlings couldn't spell worth a tinker's damn. Miss Merrihew considered that the handwriting of a female of distinction should be elegant first, legible second, and accurate a negligible third. The young ladies in Rosellen's care treated spelling as a creative exercise. St. Peter would look over Rosellen's life on Judgment Day and see the spelling errors.

Now it was too late to make a better impression. Miss Merrihew had even deemed Rosellen past praying for, sending her cleric brother instead to pray over Lady Mary in the next bed. Of course. Lady Mary's father was a duke; he'd gladly pay for the Reverend Mr. Merrihew's reverences. Rosellen's own vicar father, who had cheerfully prayed for and prayed with his penniless parishioners, would be spinning in his grave. Perhaps he'd put in a good word for her, for surely her kind and gentle papa had the angels' ears. Soon enough he'd have Rosellen's ear, too. Too soon.

Right now her own ears were being tormented by Mr. Merrihew's nasal monotone. No, she did not miss Mr. Merrihew's spiritual devotions, any more than she missed the lecher's swinish attentions. Devotions, hah! The cad was more devoted to sinful pleasure than to spiritual piety. If he weren't her employer's brother, Rosellen would have given him a piece of her mind long ago. Instead, all she'd managed to give him was a closed fist, the time he'd cornered her in the choir loft. If the ensuing black eye was another black mark against Miss Lockharte at the Pearly Gates, so be it. In a short life filled with remorse, that was one thing she would not regret.

"Here's your medicine now, miss," Fanny was saying. "And I brung you some barley water, too, what they had fixed for Lady Mary. She won't be needin' it now."

No, Lady Mary had prayers and a hired nurse from the village. Rosellen gladly swallowed the barley water but not the

3

laudanum. If she had one night left to live, she did not wish to pass it in a drugged state, asleep or too groggy to know her own name when the Grim Reaper called for her. Strange, but two days ago—or was it three?—Rosellen had been ready to welcome her own mortality. She'd been in the throes of the influenza then, however; she was merely dying now. Every hour seemed precious. No, she would savor the remaining time. "No laudanum," she managed to mumble.

"I don't know, miss," the maid said, shaking her head. "You needs your rest."

"No," Rosellen insisted, stronger now that her throat wasn't so parched. She'd have rest aplenty soon enough.

The harried maid foresaw another sleepless night for herself. "Miss Merrihew says you're to have it. Doctor's orders."

What did he know? The man was more used to setting broken bones than seeing souls laid to rest. "I'll be fine," she lied. "If you just hand me my lap desk."

All Rosellen had of her mother's was the cherrywood writing desk that had been carted downstairs from the attic chamber along with the rest of her possessions. No one, obviously, expected her to return to her own room.

"What do you want that old thing for now, miss?" Fanny was still holding the glass of laudanum, hoping to pour the contents down Miss Lockharte's throat so that she could get on with the rest of her duties and finally find her own bed.

"I want to write my will, that's what. I'll leave you the desk if you help me now."

"What would I want your old desk for, miss? Can't write, now, can I?"

Rosellen wasn't surprised. The girl had been at Miss Merrihew's for only four years. "I'm sorry. I would have taught you."

"Whatever for? So's I could become one of the teachers like you?"

The look on the maid's face expressed what she thought of Miss Lockharte's advantages over her own position.

4

"My red cloak then, which you've always admired. I'll leave you that in my will if you hand me the desk and bring the candle closer."

Fanny just clucked her tongue at the foibles of the gentry, but she did as Rosellen requested, propping the young woman up with pillows and setting the wood desk across her knees. "I'll be leavin' the laudanum here, iffen you change your mind."

Rosellen wouldn't. She had too much to accomplish in too short a time. As soon as Fanny left, she opened the desk and withdrew paper, pen, and ink. Then she decided she wasn't up to quills and blotters. She found a sharpened pencil. At least Miss Merrihew never stinted on writing materials for the penmanship instructor. Rosellen wrote *Last Will and Testament* across the top of a clean page. Then she stopped to think. Other than her desk and cloak, she had nothing anyone would want, and no one to leave it to anyway. She did, however, have a lot to say. She crossed out *Last Will and*. She would leave the testimony of her short life as her final bequest.

She had made mistakes along the way, Rosellen freely admitted. Who could claim that he or she hadn't? Yet most of Miss Lockharte's misfortunes, including this gravest—hah!—one of all, were not of her making. At this point she had nothing to lose by laying the blame where it belonged. In fact, she told herself, by expressing her anger and resentment, she might gain some peace for her soul. It couldn't be good to arrive in Heaven with such a large chip on her shoulder. There'd be no room for wings.

On the other hand, who would read the maudlin ramblings of an insignificant instructress? No one. Rosellen crossed out *Testament*. She'd write letters instead. That way, she was sure those people who had set her, willy-nilly, on this path to perdition at a girls' school would learn of her demise. Perhaps they might even regret their contribution to her downfall. She told herself she didn't want anyone to shed tears for her, nor to feel guilty, but if any of her tormentors felt the slightest twinge, perhaps they would change their ways. What was good for her soul might improve another's. Miss Lockharte's last letters just might benefit someone else. That's what she told herself, anyway.

Rosellen chewed on the pencil, something she'd forbidden her students to do, while she decided where to start. She couldn't blame dear Papa for leaving her unprovided for and unprotected. He'd done his best. Besides, she'd see him soon enough, by her figuring, alongside the mother she barely remembered and the baby brother she never got to know at all. No, she'd start with Mama's brother, Baron Haverhill.

Dear Uncle Townsend, she began. *I am dying, and I never had a waltz or a dog or a family Christmas.* She'd had happy Christmases in St. Jerome's old vicarage before her mother died, when the parishioners could spare a goose or, later, when Squire Pemberly remembered to invite the widowed vicar and his daughter to the party for his tenant farmers. She'd had gingerbread and Christmas puddings and wassail with the carolers, but she'd never had a celebration with her only relatives, at Haverhill Hall. When she first came to Miss Merrihew's, she'd heard the students chatter of their holiday plans, the great gatherings, the huge feasts, the joyous celebrations that went on through New Year's to Twelfth Night. That was when she'd realized what she'd missed, what her mother must have missed in the years at the vicarage.

Uncle Townsend had never forgiven his sister, Margaret, for marrying a poor clergyman instead of the wealthy nobleman he'd selected for her. She had made her bed, he firmly believed, so she could lie in it, in the drafty manse of an impoverished parish, on thrice-darned sheets, without any help or notice from her wealthy family.

It wasn't the money that would have made such a difference in their lives, Rosellen wrote, although William Lockharte was a parson who practiced what he preached by giving away most of his meager living to his needier congregation. The absence of kinship, the sense of belonging, was more hurtful. Her mother would not have been so careworn, Rosellen believed, if she'd not been disregarded by her only brother. Vicar Lockharte would not have felt such a failure, dragging a peer's sister to a pockets-to-let parsonage. Lud only knew if Mama would have survived the childbirthing if she'd had more nourishing food or a maid to help with the laundry and the housekeeping. But Rosellen was not blaming her uncle, she carefully explained in her letter. Her parents had loved each other very much, and they had both known what sacrifices they would have to make. She didn't even blame him for not coming to her mother's funeral. She perfectly understood how, having ignored his own sister in life, he'd felt he had no place at her grave site. Rosellen admired him for not being a hypocrite. He was coldhearted and closedminded but not a hypocrite.

And he had given Rosellen a Season in London. She thanked Uncle Townsend anew. Of course Papa'd had to humble himself to write to his brother-in-law, almost begging the baron to take her for the few months. Vicar Lockharte had seen no other way of providing for his daughter's future except by putting her in the vicinity of marriageable gentlemen, ones who did not smell of sheep pens, like the few widowers or old bachelors in his own flock. And of course Uncle Townsend had begrudgingly extended the invitation with the proviso that Rosellen make herself useful to her vaporish aunt and her demanding cousin.

Surely it wasn't Uncle Townsend's fault that Aunt Beatrice had never exerted herself to introduce Rosellen to any halfway eligible *partis*. Nor could he have supposed that Cousin Clarice and her cattish friends would ridicule Rosellen's countrified manners, her outmoded dress, and her vicar's-daughter virtues. Rosellen was not condemning her uncle, she wrote, for London's low morals or for the fact that she hadn't stayed long enough to receive permission to waltz from those old tabbies at Almack's.

He could, however, have asked Rosellen for her explanation about that disastrous evening at Lady Maplethorpe's ball. He could have trusted that she would not have gone out on the balcony with a hey-go-mad young cavalry officer without good reason. He could have had faith in Vicar Lockharte's daughter not to let an inebriated stranger kiss her. Uncle Townsend could have done all those things, but he had not. He'd listened to Clarice instead, spiteful, jealous, vain Clarice who'd engineered the entire debacle rather than share the least of her beaux. Then he'd declared Rosellen wanton and ruined. She'd been a bad influence on his daughter, a threat to his wife's equilibrium, and a disgrace to her mother's memory. She'd also been on a public coach the next morning.

Uncle Townsend did secure a position for her at Miss Merrihew's, Clarice's old school. What Miss Merrihew might have taught the self-absorbed shrew was a mystery to Rosellen, for Clarice never spoke of aught but fashions, flirtations, and finding the highest-titled, deepest-pocketed fiancé. Despite such a poor recommendation, Rosellen accepted the post of handwriting instructor rather than return to the vicarage, a drain on her father's slim resources, a disappointment to his hopes.

Rosellen did not hold Baron Haverhill responsible for Miss Merrihew's refusal to let her return home to nurse her father in his last hours, she continued on a second sheet. No, she thanked him now for his efforts on her behalf. She was sorry she had embarrassed him in the social world he and his family inhabited. She'd try her best to look after them all when she got to Heaven, as she had every expectation of doing, since she was not a fallen woman despite certain persons' accusations and appearances to the contrary. She did hope, however, that Uncle Townsend would not be quite so quick to judge others in the future or, barring that, that he not sit as magistrate in his home borough. And could he please see that she was buried next to her parents in St. Jerome's churchyard, next to the manse where she'd been raised?

Rosellen folded the letter, then tipped the candle to make a drip of wax to seal it. She felt years younger, pounds lighter, having given expression to her spleen. She felt so much relieved, in fact, that she took out her quill and bottle of ink to address the front of the letter in her best copperplate. There, let Uncle Townsend see that she wasn't an entirely ignorant female, like some she could mention if she weren't a vicar's daughter with hopes of Heaven. Then she sharpened the point on her pencil and smoothed out a fresh sheet of paper. *Dear Cousin Clarice,* she wrote. *I am dying, and I never wore a silk gown.*

Chapter Two

*T*en thousand silkworms had spun their little hearts out for Clarice. Her closets and clothespresses were filled with gossamer gowns in every color. She also had satins and sarcenets, laces and lutestrings, fabrics Rosellen had barely heard of, much less seen or touched. Seeing and touching was all she got to do, fetching for her cousin. Clarice had a fancy French lady's maid, of course, but she enjoyed having her cousin wait on her, lest the country rustic start putting on airs. The country rustic got to put on Clarice's discarded muslins from her debutante days, at her uncle's insistence. Aunt Beatrice had refused to be seen with such a dowd, declaring that the French maid dressed better than this unwanted chit. Uncle Townsend had refused to expend another groat on his sister's brat when his own poppet had more gowns than she could wear.

The castoffs were white, all of them, with the trims long removed for use on other frocks. Clarice was raven-haired and rosy-complected. She must have looked stunning in those demure colorless gowns. Rosellen had looked like a ghost. With her sandy hair and pale skin, not even her turquoise eyes— quite her best feature, she always thought—could bring life to unrelieved white. She might have been wearing bedsheets.

Rosellen had tried tucking flowers in the necklines, from the bouquets Clarice received daily, until she saw how the flowers drooped and faded during the interminable evenings of sitting on the sidelines at one ball or another, watching Clarice dance by on the arms of her handsome beaux. Her bedsheets would have been welcome.

Uncle's next suggestion had been for Clarice to pick out a horse from the stables for Rosellen, so the cousins might ride together at the fashionable hour, where the vicar's undowered daughter might catch the eye of some well-heeled gentleman. Rosellen would have caught flies quicker. Clarice had made sure that her poor relation was mounted on the slowest plug she could find, one that couldn't possibly keep up with her and her friends on their high-bred, spirited Thoroughbreds. Rosellen had stopped riding in the park at about the same time she had stopped trying to prettify her white gowns. What had been the point?

Uncle had also insisted that Clarice introduce Rosellen to her circle of admirers. Clarice had duly presented her to all her suitors with spots, stutters, squints, and skimpy finances. None of the marriage-minded could afford a wife of no income. Leg-shackles were fine, so long as they were made of gold. Half-pay officers, aged libertines, hardened gamblers, and anyone else of no use to Clarice were also sent Rosellen's way. As soon as these so-called gentlemen found out that the vicar's daughter would not play their sophisticated games in dark corners, she was back on a gilded chair against the wall, as dispirited as her drooping flowers.

Rosellen had been so excited about going to London. She was to be welcomed by her mother's exalted relatives, see the sights, meet the man of her dreams. He'd cherish her forever and look after Papa in his retirement. Hunched over her writing desk, she frowned now at her own näiveté then. She shrugged her thin shoulders. She'd been seventeen and away from home for the first time in her life. What could be more wondrous than being introduced to the *haut monde* under her beautiful cousin's aegis? Falling off the barn roof, that's what.

Clarice had been nineteen, the reigning Toast of the last two London Seasons. She'd won accolades and offers but none elevated enough for her to accept. She had quickly gained a reputation as a heartless jade, hard to please, and hot-at-hand. In two days Rosellen had realized that the Diamond of the First Water had ditchwater in her veins.

Rosellen sharpened her pencil again while she thought some more. Clarice was not entirely to blame for her faults, of course. Her very beauty was her greatest handicap. The Incomparable Miss Haverhill had been raised to be her father's prized possession, her faded mother's restored youth and looks. So what if she'd been her nanny's nightmare, her governesses' grief? The baron and his wife never had to deal with Clarice's tantrums. They never noticed the crying maids, the broken crockery, the winded horses. To ensure their continued ignorance of the harridan they'd raised, Aunt Beatrice kept to her bed and Uncle Townsend kept to his clubs. No wonder they'd hoped Rosellen might prove a good influence on their daughter. Pigs would fly first.

Not content to hold her cousin up to ridicule among her own friends, Clarice had set out to ruin her. Perhaps Miss Lockharte had had a holier-than-thou attitude toward Clarice and her rackety circle. She'd apologize for that in her letter. Then again, perhaps Clarice hadn't approved of her cousin's making friends with the other wallflowers or some of her rejected suitors. Maybe Rosellen hadn't been quite the antidote, once the French maid had given her some silk flowers and a bit of ribbon to trim the gowns and put in her hair. Either way, Clarice had wanted her cousin out of her house, out of London. She'd known enough rotters and rag-mannered rascals to see the deed done and witnessed by half the ton.

From her viewpoint at death's door, Rosellen couldn't see where her cousin had benefited. Clarice was now twenty-two and still unwed. What Rosellen gathered from her students' gossip was that Clarice Haverhill was deemed a confirmed fortune hunter. No one held husband hunting against a female; that's why they all went to London in the first place. But the *belle monde* did frown on those who reached above themselves. Clarice was standing on tiptoe. She was also standing perilously close to the shelf by London standards.

Rosellen didn't write any of this, of course. Considering that Clarice had been educated at Miss Merrihew's Select Academy, Rosellen doubted her cousin could read, much less between the lines. What she did write was of her true regrets that the two of them couldn't have been friends. Rosellen added that she hoped Clarice found her heart's content—beyond finding the perfect bonnet—before it was too late. She promised to look down fondly on the only cousin she was ever to have, even if they'd never rubbed along well together. And yes, she forgave Clarice for the white dresses, the slow horses, and the chinless callers. She even, Rosellen ended with a flourish, forgave her cousin for the melodrama at Lady Maplethorpe's. Clarice couldn't have known that Rosellen would end up at Miss Merrihew's, dying alone in a damp and dirty nightgown in a dormitory of dimwitted debutantes.

That was magnanimous of her, Rosellen decided, resting back on her pillows. And forgiveness was definitely divine, for she felt immeasurably better once Clarice's letter was sealed and addressed. She felt light-headed, in fact. Perhaps that was the fever, or the lack of nourishment, or the course of her illness. Knowing she had no time to spare for idle thoughts, Rosellen took out a fresh sheet of paper and wrote, *Dear sir, I am dying, and I never had a dog.* She would not address this letter to the Honorable Timothy Heatherstone, nor the similar one she intended to copy for his twin brother, the Honorable Thomas Heatherstone, for she did not consider these two makebates to be honorable at all. London considered the Heatherstone lads regular goers, cheerful pranksters, and choice spirits, up to every rig and row. Rosellen considered the identical redheads fribbles. They were two gudgeons with one freckled face and one feckless brain between them. Papa would have disapproved of the twins as peep-o'-day boys, reckless sportsmen and reckless gamblers. They were two of the so-called gentlemen who had aided Clarice to ruin her cousin on a bet.

Part of the beauty's court, the twins had seemed innocuous at first. After they played their silly game of changing identities, they'd ignored Miss Haverhill's poor relation until the night of the Maplethorpe ball. Then one of them, Heaven only knew which, or cared, came to find Rosellen, where she occupied yet another uncomfortable gilt chair on the edge of the dance floor. Clarice needed her, the Heatherstone halfwit claimed, out on the terrace. Rosellen never questioned what her cousin might be doing on the terrace or why her aunt hadn't been called from the card room or a footman delegated to carry Clarice to safety, or any of a thousand questions she should have asked, in much wiser hindsight. But she was a parson's daughter, used to serving, used to giving aid in emergencies.

The interchangeable Heatherstone hurried her out of the ballroom, down the stairs, and toward the library at the rear of Maplethorpe House. There, French doors opened onto the paved terrace, where lanterns were strung in the trees to mark benches and paths. Rosellen couldn't see Clarice.

"Under the balcony," Timothy or Thomas urged, pointing her in that direction but not following. Clarice wasn't there either, but a castaway cornet was, his swaying scarlet regimental jacket like an exotic flower blooming under the lantern light in Lady Maplethorpe's garden. He seemed to think that Rosellen had left the ball, left the chaperones, and left her morals behind, just for him.

"Knew you'd come, sweetings. Been waiting all night."

Still concerned for her cousin, Rosellen never considered her own safety. She merely pushed past the officer, looking for Clarice.

He grabbed her wrist. "Not so fast, little bird. I'll have a kiss first," the soldier slurred.

"Do not be absurd, sir. I am looking for my cousin, not a

flirtation. You should ask Lady Maplethorpe's butler for some coffee if you are too foxed to tell a proper female from one who meets gentlemen in dark corners."

"You're here, ain't you?" That seemed proof enough for the knave, for he pulled on her arm until she was against his chest, like an angler reeling in a reluctant trout. Rosellen didn't want to scream, to draw attention to the awkward situation, but she did beat against his arm and try to kick at his shins. He was wearing high boots. She was wearing paper-thin dancing slippers. For all the dancing she'd been doing, she'd have been better off in her riding boots. For all the good her struggling did, she'd have been better off saving her breath for when he kissed her. That way she wouldn't have had to smell the sour wine fumes emanating from her assailant.

A scream ended the assault, but it wasn't Rosellen's shout. It was Clarice's, from the ballroom balcony directly overhead. Scores of guests rushed to her side, to see the Haverhill country cousin in the arms of a notorious womanizer, Lieutenant Roland Dawe.

Before her uncle came and dragged her away, a benumbed Rosellen did hear both Heatherstone brothers congratulate their friend. "Clarice swore you'd never get a kiss out of Miss Prunes and Prisms, Rolly. Here's the monkey we owe you. Good show."

Her downfall had been entertainment for those dirty dishes, costly but amusing. Rosellen felt no compunction about taking a bit of pleasure herself, thinking of the discomfort she hoped her letters might cause. She wrote that she forgave the brothers for their contribution to her short, tragic life. Papa would be proud of her generosity. He'd be less pleased when she concluded both letters with the threat of coming back to haunt the Heatherstones if they ever, *ever*, brought dishonor on another female.

Rosellen didn't really believe in ghosts, but who knew? Certainly not those featherheaded Heatherstone twins.

If anyone deserved to be besieged by bogeys from the

beyond, it was Lieutenant Dawe. He had laughed when Uncle Townsend demanded a proposal of marriage.

"What are you going to do, Baron, call me out if I don't offer for the chit? She came out to the terrace by herself, you know. Who's to say I was the first?"

Having seen the lieutenant pocket the money, then exchange winks with Clarice, Rosellen found it almost impossible to forgive the officer. She wrote that she would try, for the sake of her immortal soul and his. *I am dying,* she wrote, *and I shall never have known a kiss from a man who loves me, thanks to your machinations.* Surely there was a special place in Hell for sinners like him. She'd look into it, if Dawe didn't change his devil-may-care ways. Old Nick mightn't care how many innocent young women the lieutenant ruined, but Rosellen Lockharte definitely did. If not for him and that foul, fetid kiss, she'd never have ended up at Miss Merrihew's Select Academy for Young Females of Distinction. And extinction.

Now *there* was a letter Rosellen was literally dying to write. *Dear Miss Merrihew, I am dying, and I never held a child of my own.* She'd held the younger girls when they were crying with homesickness, the older ones when they would have torn each other's hair out. But that was not the same. Perhaps Miss Merrihew wouldn't care about Rosellen's unfulfilled maternal instincts, since the old harpy seemed to have none herself. Rosellen crossed out the line rather than begin on a fresh sheet. She was running out of paper as well as time. *Dear Miss Merrihew, I am dying and I never had a paid vacation.*

First she thanked the dried-up old stick for giving a young, untried instructor a position. For six months, on trial, without pay. Who knew what would have happened to Rosellen otherwise? She might have gone home to her father, married one of the local sheepherders, and lived another forty years. Then she thanked Miss Merrihew for not giving her leave to visit her ailing papa. Rosellen couldn't have afforded the coach fare anyway and might have been accosted on the highways. The gray uniform that came out of her salary, the mandatory poor-box donation, the coal for the teachers' sitting room that was mined from their wages, Rosellen thanked her employer for them all and felt better about herself than she had in years. She even thanked the clutch-fisted crone for moving her to the attic room after Rosellen had tried to better her position. The room was freezing in winter, stifling in summer, and too low-ceilinged for her to stand in, though the single, ill-fitting round window did have a lovely view of the school's fenced-in rear yard.

Her employment at the school had consisted of "Yes, Miss Merrihew" and "No, Miss Merrihew." Rosellen was amazed she had a tongue left after biting down on it to keep the angry words from spewing forth. Well, no more. She had nothing to lose by telling Miss Mirabel Merrihew that she was a cheese-paring chowderhead who knew less about educating young women than Rosellen knew about electricity.

For two pages Rosellen wrote, ignoring the commotion on the other side of the screen. She turned the sheets over and scrawled two more pages about how a proper school should be run, right down to the quality of meats served at table, the sanitary conditions of the kitchens, the books in the library, and the moral virtues that should be part of every young lady's education. Why, if the parents of Miss Merrihew's students ever found out how little their daughters were actually taught or how likely they were to suffer from food poisoning, they'd never send them. They would certainly never enroll their daughters, she concluded, if they knew Miss Merrihew's scurvy brother paid calls after dark, and not to say prayers either. That attic room *did* have a good view.

I am dying, Mr. Merrihew, and I never got to see the prince. The other teachers got to lead class trips to Brighton or to chaperon students to their summer homes during the long vacation. Not Rosellen. The Reverend Mr. Merrihew had convinced his sister that Miss Lockharte was too immature, too irresponsible for such plums. Too unapproachable, more like. Rosellen's conditions at the academy had deteriorated from unpleasant to unbearable after she had rebuffed the caddish cleric's advances. When she died, she was going to watch out for the other girls at the school, Rosellen warned that son of pond scum now. She'd make sure he didn't sneak any more schoolgirls out at night as he'd done to poor Vivian Baldour, who'd been sent home in disgrace. Miss Baldour, Rosellen had heard, was hurriedly married off to the Earl of Comfrey, a man who was older than her father.

My dear Lady Comfrey, I hope this finds you in better straits than mine. I wish to beg your pardon for not protecting your innocence more vehemently whilst you were in my charge. I hope you find happiness and fulfillment in your marriage. Miss Baldour would have been better off with a chimney sweep than she'd been with Mr. Merrihew, whose aim seemed to be to compromise some wealthy chit into an advantageous marriage. Advantageous for him, at least. Miss Baldour's father was too downy, or the Earl of Comfrey was too eager to get an heir, one way or the other. The girl shouldn't have had to suffer for falling for a rake's practiced promises, and him in holy orders! Papa would have been aghast.

Her pencil was nearly down to the nub and she didn't have another in the desk, but Rosellen wasn't finished yet. *Dear Lord Vance,* she wrote, trying not to press so firmly on the page, *I am dying, and I never even owned a dog.* She knew she was repeating herself, but she was growing weary. Besides, Lord Vance, one of the school's local patrons, was a sportsman with his own pack of hounds. He'd understand, but Rosellen could not fathom what the man was doing calling after midnight through the back gate. Her little round window revealed him tying his horse behind some trees, then skulking through the shrubbery. Whatever the man was doing, it couldn't be any good. If he thought that the heavenly hosts knew of his clandestine visits to Miss Merrihew's rooms, perhaps he'd stay at home with his wife. At the least, he should consult mad King George's physicians. Miss Merrihew, indeed!

By the close of Lord Vance's letter, Rosellen was yawning, struggling to keep her eyes open. Not yet, she begged, not yet. She had two more letters to complete before she could write *finis* to her life.

Chapter Three

My dear Susan, I could not leave this mortal plane without bidding you farewell. I might never have had a beau or a babe or seen a balloon ascension, but I did have a friend. Here Rosellen had to stop to blow her nose and blot a fallen tear from the paper. She could hardly see what she had written, through the moisture in her eyes and the ever-increasing weakness. Her fingers were numb and cold. Just a little longer, she begged whoever might be listening. Attila the Hun lived to be over forty; surely Rosellen the Writing Instructor could be granted another hour.

Miss Susan Alton was the only girl at Miss Merrihew's to befriend Rosellen when she arrived at the school. Kindness seemed the rarest commodity at the academy, scarcer even than a decent meal, until Susan smiled at her. Mere months apart in age, they were worlds apart in upbringing, yet Susan was not too proud to accept the disgraced parson's brat as a companion. Granddaughter to a duke, sister to a viscount, Susan was used to the ways of Society and refused to permit gossip and innuendoes to color her affection. The bumblebroth at the Maplethorpe ball could have happened to any green girl, Susan swore, especially one without a mama to advise her or a male guardian to protect her. Susan had her brother, Wynn, and was sure no here-and-thereian would trifle with her affections or her honor whilst the formidable Viscount Stanford was nearby breathing malevolence and loading his Mantons.

Perhaps gentle Susan's kindness was the cruelest rub of all, for she'd offered hope and handed Rosellen heartbreak. When Rosellen had been at Miss Merrihew's for six months, Susan Alton had already been there for two years. She was looking forward to her come-out that spring. Rosellen had nothing to look forward to but at least two score more years of drudgery and disrespect. She'd grow old and ink-stained, her gnarled fingers permanently curled around a pen, her voice coarsened by a lifetime of carping, "Ladies, mind your uprights."

But Susan had an idea. Her mother was an invalid, especially when it suited her to cry off from dreary musicales and mandatory morning calls. The Dowager Viscountess Stanford was still a leading light in the *belle monde*, but she was not up to accompanying her young daughter to museums and libraries and shops, picnics to Richmond, or boat rides to Vauxhall. Susan was going to need a companion, and who better to fill the position than her own dear Miss Lockharte?

Rosellen was in alt. Not only would she escape the penny-pinching of her employer and the petty meanness of the other instructors, but she'd have hope again, hope of a life for herself. She'd be in London, where anything was possible. Oh, she didn't dream that some wealthy peer would take one look at her turquoise eyes—her only claim to glory, actually—and declare himself smitten. No, Society gentlemen were too far above her touch and too low in her esteem, after her last encounter with the breed of care-for-naughts. She thought only to find herself in the vicinity of a clerk or a secretary or a younger son, anyone who might wish a good housekeeper, a loyal wife, a loving mother for his children. He needn't be wealthy or titled or well placed in the ton. Rosellen's requirements were simple: the gentleman had to be kind, with a modicum of learning, and he had to be able to afford a wife.

Was that asking too much? Rosellen didn't think so, and neither did Susan, who promised there were scads of such likely candidates in the vicinity of Stanford House, Grosvenor Square. Her brother had contacts with the War Office, with his investment bankers, with his estate managers. Her mother knew everyone else.

If not, Susan swore, if every man in London was deaf, dumb, or poor, Rosellen could stay on with her as the young lady's paid companion. Then she could be governess to the five children Susan wanted, after Miss Alton found her own Sir Lancelot. *He,* naturally, would be everything Rosellen's humble *parti* was not: well born and well breeched. And devastatingly attractive, Susan insisted. Rosellen wasn't sure about the five children, or the emphasis her friend was putting on the gentleman's outward appearance instead of his inner character, but she didn't care. So long as he could afford to pay her fair wages, enough that she might have a pension and a cottage of her own someday, Susan could marry a troll. A nice troll, of course, for sweet Susan deserved no less.

Rosellen was like a parched wanderer lost in the desert. Susan was the guide pointing toward the oasis. Except the water hole disappeared when Rosellen approached it. Was Susan's affection just a mirage then? Rosellen didn't want to believe so. It was easier to accept that Miss Alton was a pretty widgeon with more hair than wit. Susan hadn't foreseen any problems, but she hadn't an ounce of intellect. Rosellen hadn't remembered that when she gave her notice to Miss Merrihew and packed her bag. And Susan hadn't remembered that she needed her brother's approval before hiring a companion.

The viscount had arrived to fetch his sister home from school in a great flurry of outriders, with Miss Merrihew curtsying so low, her brother had to haul her back to her feet. With one wave of his manicured hand, the viscount ordered the bags packed. With another wave he declined to take tea with the toadying twosome. With a third and final flick of his lace-edged wrist, he dismissed his sister's new companion.

"Absurd" was all he said, with a sneer, before turning his caped back on Miss Lockharte and all her aspirations. She might have been an ant on his picnic cloth, a speck of lint on his elegant superfine sleeve. She might have been the dust beneath his feet in the academy's courtyard for all the notice he gave. He didn't say she was too young, too inexperienced, too unworldly. He didn't know that her reputation was tarnished. He didn't care. "Absurd." He'd been able to destroy her life with one word. Now that *was* absurd.

To her credit, Susan had argued with the arrogant aristocrat. "But, Wynn, I'll be all alone in London, with no friends. Miss Lockharte will be excellent company."

"Don't be ridiculous, brat. We're related to half the ton. Now get in the coach. I am meeting friends at Epsom."

In shock, Rosellen wondered if Lord Stanford had an appointment to gamble away enough blunt to feed her father's parish for a lifetime, including the sheep. Or perhaps the impatient peer was going to rendezvous with his mistress and shower her with diamonds and rubies.

Susan could only wave her white handkerchief out the carriage window and swear she'd write. Rosellen could only stare after the departing coach, there in the carriage drive, amid her shattered dreams and her belongings. All she possessed fit into a satchel, and her mother's writing desk, which she clutched to herself now, as a talisman. She had no money, no references, and no position left at Miss Merrihew's.

Susan hadn't acted out of malice, Rosellen knew. She was simply weak and a woman. Susan hadn't stood up for Rosellen; now she was in danger of succumbing to another of her guardian's dictates. Rosellen's hurriedly penciled letter exhorted Miss Alton to be strong-willed on her own behalf, lest that same overbearing brother force her into an unwanted marriage. The contemptuous cad had ruined Rosellen's life; she didn't want to see him destroy Susan's future also.

No, Susan Alton had not been intentionally cruel. Her brother, Viscount Stanford, was another story altogether. Rosellen would never forgive his toplofty lordship, no, not even if her soul burned in Hell for all of eternity for showing no mercy. She'd meet the dastard there, she trusted, and tell him what she thought of such arrant disregard for the feelings of others, such arrogant uninterest in the lives of those less blessed. But why wait till Judgment Day to tell Viscount Stanford that she thought he was slime?

Rosellen might have been beneath his haughtiness's notice that day in the courtyard, but she'd get his attention now, in her final letter. Her pencil was worn so small, she could barely hold it in her numb fingers. With shaking hands she unstoppered the bottle of ink and sharpened her quill. She'd rather plunge the penknife in the varlet's black heart, she thought, but giving Viscount Stanford a piece of her mind—the last piece—was the best she could do. If he had any brains at all, and someone in that wealthy, influential family must, she considered, he'd mend his ways. Perhaps Susan would reap some of the benefits.

The penmanship wasn't her finest. Hours away from the Hereafter, what else was to be expected? If that sneering Stanford had to squint to read her letter, maybe he'd understand how low she'd had to grovel to regain her position at the school. Her knees must still have scars. Only she hadn't regained her position at all. Another teacher had already been hired, Miss Merrihew reported with a smirk, and had been given Rosellen's bed in the room she'd shared with the French instructor. Of course there was the attic cubby, and Miss Merrihew supposed she could use a penmanship teacher for the younger girls, at less pay, naturally.

Rosellen had had no choice. Her father was gone; another family had moved into the vicarage. Her uncle refused to have a fallen woman under his roof, and her dreams had driven away in a crested carriage. She crawled, all the way up to the attic room, cursing the vainglorious viscount with every step.

If not for him, she wrote, she wouldn't have been garreted in a freezing closet, where she'd gotten a chill, which had left her susceptible to the influenza epidemic that was now claiming her life. Could he forgive himself for killing an innocent woman in her prime? Rosellen couldn't. Let her death be a burden to him forever, she told him, a weighted reminder that power corrupts. *Noblesse oblige be damned,* she wrote, leaving a small blot on the page. *Vive la revolution.*

The ink ran out before Rosellen's strength, thank goodness. She managed to push the lap desk off her knees and gather the letters into a pile on the nightstand before collapsing back onto the pillows. There, she had accomplished something. Now all she had to do was hang on till morning, which couldn't be all that far away. Rosellen didn't think she could do it. Her eyes drifted shut.

How sad, she wasn't going to last long enough to see her letters posted, for shining through her closed lids came the light she'd always heard about, come to lead her upward.

"Here, miss, I've pulled the curtains for you so's you can see what a pretty day it is. Sunshine'll make you feel more the thing."

Strange, Rosellen had always imagined dying at night or in the rain or at least on a gray, gloomy day. She could manage only a grunt, which seemed enough for Fanny.

"I looked in twice durin' the night, but you was so busy with your scribblin' you never noticed. Th' doctor was too busy to ask iffen you'd had your laudanum, so I guess it didn't matter none. Didn't do no harm, that I can see."

"Any," Rosellen corrected, schoolteacher to the end. She found that she could talk more easily, once she'd sipped at the lukewarm tea the maid had brought. "I need to ask a favor of you, Fanny."

"Oh, I don't know, miss, we're still at sixes and sevens after last night. Miss Merrihew is like to sleep in this morning, thank goodness, else I don't know how we'd get everything done before she's up and giving the staff more orders. I don't have no spare time to be bringin' you bathwater or nothin'."

It would be lovely to greet her parents with clean hair and a fresh nightgown, Rosellen thought, her mind wandering. "No, that's not what I want. I just wish you to see that my letters get posted."

Fanny wrinkled her forehead. "I couldn't do that, Miss Lockharte. You know as how Miss Merrihew has to look over all the young ladies' mail."

"But I'm not a young lady, Fanny. That is, I'm not one of the students. Besides, half of the letters stay right here. You could get the egg man to take the one for Lord Vance."

"Lord Vance what leases mistress the property for her school? Lud, what truck do you have with the likes of him, Miss Lockharte?"

"Nothing that concerns you. You simply need to ask one of the delivery boys to carry my letter along with him. And take the others to the posting house. Most go to London except Lady Comfrey's. Do you remember Vivian Baldour who married that old man? I believe she is in Bath, where her gout-ridden spouse is taking the waters."

"I hear he's worth an abbey."

Rosellen wasn't interested in the latest gossip. "All that matters is that Vivian will be able to pay for the post. Uncle Townsend and Lord Stanford can well stand the expense, too."

Fanny was scratching her head. "I'm sorry, Miss Lockharte, but it'd mean my job, was th' mistress to hear of such goings-on. Writin' to Lord Stanford, by all that's holy."

"There is nothing holy about that dreadful man, Fanny."

"Lud, don't I just know it. I only saw him but once or twice, when he escorted his sister comin' or goin'. But I swear his eyes alone could lead a girl down the primrose path."

"His eyes were hard and cold, and I don't have time to argue."

"What, are you going somewhere?" Fanny laughed at her own joke.

Rosellen didn't think it all that funny. "The viscount's is the most important letter of all. I cannot go in peace till I know he'll get it."

"I knew you should have had the drops. You've gone and taken the fever again, haven't you?"

Rosellen couldn't tell and didn't care. What did it matter anyway? "I'll take the laudanum now, Fanny, if you'll just see that the letters get posted. I have a few coins to pay the delivery boy and the driver. If any is left, you can keep it for your own." Rosellen wouldn't be needing her paltry life savings. "And remember, I promised you my red cloak. Take it and go now before Miss Merrihew comes to breakfast, so you'll be warm on the way to the posting house. She'll never know, and I'll rest easy."

The maid had visions of walking to church on Sunday in that lovely wool cape. Sam, the butcher's boy, couldn't ignore her then, not by half. "I'll do it, miss, iffen you're sure that's how you want to spend your blunt."

"I've never been more certain. Here, I'll mark the outsides so that you can tell which go where. See, these two have black marks. They're for Miss Merrihew and her brother. The one with the smudged address is Lord Vance's. The rest go to the receiving office."

"An' you'll take the laudanum so's no one can say you went without?"

"Yes, I'm ready now." And she was, drained of her anger, drained of her strength to hold back the tides of fate. She swallowed the bitter dose and watched Fanny put her precious letters in her apron pocket, along with Rosellen's thin purse. Then she watched the sun rise in the sky until her vision blurred and there were two bright lights instead of one. Her eyes drifted shut. Now the lights danced behind her lids, in the waltz she'd never had.

Rosellen took a deep breath. This was not a bad way to die, if one had to die.

Chapter Four

To Wynn Alton, Viscount Stanford, Stanford House, Grosvenor Square, London, he read. *Sir, I am dying and I never had a dog.* What in the blazes? Wynn thought, his eyes glancing through another sentence or two, then traveling down the page to the signature on the bottom. Bloody hell, just what he needed, more misplaced melodrama. Miss Loveharte? Lostheart? He couldn't tell, from the blots on the page. Miss Lonely Heart, he surmised, a female past her last prayers trying to gain his attention. She'd catch cold at that game, Wynn swore. Better women than this upstart had tried to snabble themselves an eligible peer. Devil take it, he didn't even know the blasted female. For sure he didn't know any woman who would label one of London's premier bachelors an insect. It was a novel approach, he had to admit, tossing the letter onto the trash pile. If there was one thing he didn't need, however, it was another hysterical female. This one sounded like an old biddy with nothing to do except complain about her health and try to make him responsible for every hangnail and headache. He was already responsible for enough high-strung females without taking on strangers, by George.

Sometimes Wynn felt like Atlas, with the weight of the world on his shoulders. He could manage the weight, he thought, if he weren't standing in quicksand. He brushed back his dark hair in a gesture that was more habit than necessity. He was up to his neck in nuisances, and it wasn't even lunchtime.

First there'd been Maude, his mistress. Except that he didn't want a mistress anymore. That is, his mother had brought home to him how his licentiousness was a bad influence on his sister. He was one of the most discreet, fastidious men he knew, so how his mother was even aware of Maude's existence was a mystery to him. Further, Wynn couldn't see how the actions of an unencumbered gentleman of mature years affected the behavior of a silly chit attending debutante balls, but he did not argue with his mother. An upset Lady Stanford suffered paroxysms. After thirty years, Wynn still had no idea what, precisely, a paroxysm consisted of, but his father had lived in dread of them. Besides, the dowager informed him, she never closed her eyes until he was home at night, so his tomcatting was sure to be the death of her. No matter that his chambers were on the opposite end of the house from the dowager's, nor that she usually resided in Bath or at the family seat in Bedford, she swore she knew when her firstborn wasn't tucked safely in his bed. Wynn was not deceived for a moment into thinking his mother lost a minute's sleep over his whereabouts. She wanted to see him wed and would go to any extremes to further her cause, right down to having one of her attacks. Since Lady Stanford was already confined to a wheelchair, how could a dutiful son cause his mother more agony? Especially when he was tiring of the opera dancer anyway?

Maude hadn't quite understood. Either that or she preferred rubies to diamonds as a parting gift. Perhaps he should have made his announcement before enjoying her favors, he acknowledged now. Something about diamonds and damp sheets did not fit. Maude had thrown a fit when he announced he wouldn't be coming back to the little house in Kensington. Then she'd thrown a vase, a perfume bottle, and a chair. By the time he reached Stanford House, he smelled like a bordello and looked like a prizefighter—the one who hadn't won the prize. And there was his mother, sitting in the parlor in her Bath chair with her eternal embroidery, waiting up for him. Since Cousin Lenore, the butler, two footmen, and her lady's maid had to attend the dowager, Wynn received nothing but reproachful looks. Since he was paying all of their inflated salaries, he thought he should have gotten a little sympathy. Slim chance.

Life had certainly been easier before his mother came to Town. The viscount had been his own man then, coming and going at his own whims, not tripping over aged matrons and their more ancient escorts or giggling schoolgirls and their spotted swains. That was another thing. Mother was there to fire off his sister. Why was the blasted process taking two bloody years? Lady Stanford was constantly nattering at him about starting his nursery; Susan should have had hers half filled by now.

Zeus, she'd been a pretty little thing, all pink and white and golden curls, Wynn thought fondly. She was still a devilishly attractive gel, he admitted, only now she wasn't to be comforted with a licorice drop or a ride on his pony. No, now she wanted to attend a masquerade at Vauxhall Gardens in the company of one of London's worst rakes. So what if Tully Hadfield was a boon companion of Wynn's? The blighter wasn't fit to touch Susan's skirts. In fact, if the loose screw tried to touch the chit's anything, Wynn would call him out. So he told him the night before when the rum go had had the gall to ask for Susan's hand, and so he told his sister this morning at breakfast.

He should have worn his burgundy waistcoat. It would have matched the raspberry jam better. After the broken crockery came the tears, which were worse. Hell and tarnation, why couldn't the widgeon toss her handkerchief at the friends he *wanted* her to like? Wasn't he dragging Jack Deforrest and Tripp Hayes over to Stanford House every chance he got?

They were steady and reliable, neither drinking nor gambling to excess. Either one of them would make Susan a good husband, but did she make any effort to attach their interest? No, she let Cousin Lenore make polite conversation. What the deuce was Susan looking for? She could bring either of the chaps up to scratch with the flutter of her long eyelashes. Then she'd be off setting up housekeeping, Mother would return to Bath with Lenore, her embroidery, and her insomnia, and Wynn could get his life back in order.

Women were the very devil, he thought, not for the first time, rubbing his bruised jaw. They were good for only one thing, and that in small doses so they didn't think they owned a fellow. No, he had to admit, they had another use. Mother was right; he needed an heir. The quicksand was rising or he was sinking.

And all he wanted to do was play with his toy soldiers.

They weren't toys, of course, and he didn't play. He painted them, from intricate lead castings he commissioned from his own clay models. No taller than his hand's width, they were painstakingly authentic, down to the gold braid and the ribbons on their chests and the swords at their sides. He used drawings from the War Office, or actual captured uniforms when possible, to guarantee the accuracy of his miniature French troops. That way the British soldiers knew precisely where to aim. Wynn didn't like to think of his work being used as models for decoys, spying being in ill odor and not quite the gentlemanly pursuit. Then again, painting toy soldiers wasn't the usual pastime for a peer of the realm.

Wynn had been painting the little figures since he was a boy and confined to bed with a broken leg. He'd been unhappy with the faces of his lead soldiers, so he'd begged his tutor for paints and brushes. Relieved to find something to occupy the restless youngster, the tutor had complied, and seen that an art instructor was hired besides, to further lighten his own load. Wynn proved an excellent pupil, although he refused to graduate from Lilliputian warriors to life-size portraits or landscapes. He just wanted to paint toy soldiers. He was good at it, too.

Years later, when the heir to the Stanford succession was denied permission to enter the army and fight his country's battles, Wynn had found another way to be useful. His soldiers were sent to Wellesley and Moore and Graham, whose godsons were reputed to be fond of waging mock battles. Wynn didn't know if any of the generals so much as had a godson. His miniature Marmont and Soult had other uses. Sometimes, he heard from his contact at the War Office, the placement of the little swords told the French generals' directions, or the number of tiny riflemen in the box with them told their troop strength. Other times their hollow bases were filled with minute codes. Unlike dispatches and sealed orders, no one bothered to intercept deliveries of children's playthings. And no one outside the highest office at Whitehall knew of Viscount Stanford's contribution, which suited Wynn to a cow's thumb.

He dabbled in painting, which was his excuse for the smell of turpentine and varnish that often lingered on his hands. Just for his own amusement at odd moments, he always explained with a self-deprecating laugh, nothing fit to be seen. That was why, Wynn said, he kept his studio in a locked room off his office, lest anyone see his poor efforts. Someone had seen them, however. Two of the lead legionaries had gone missing. Marching off with those particular toy soldiers was no child's prank.

The head of security at the War Office had been upset when Wynn reported the loss immediately after changing his waistcoat after breakfast, especially when he'd seen the viscount's bruised face.

"My word, is nothing safe, when a man is attacked in his own home, for toy soldiers?"

Even when Stanford told him that such was not the case, claiming he'd been sparring at Gentleman Jackson's, the bureau chief was still unhappy. The miniatures could be replicated, unlike the real soldiers they helped defend, but the ease and security of the communication could not. Worse, who knew what the enemy would do with the figures? Worse still, there was a spy in the highest ranks of army intelligence. No one else was supposed to know about Viscount Stanford's work.

He'd returned home with a new employee, one of Wellesley's injured subalterns hurriedly briefed, pretending to be Wynn's recently hired secretary. Young Stubbing might be a crack officer and an excellent detective, but he was a terrible secretary, letting two pages of claptrap from a cork-brained clunch arrive on Wynn's desk. Besides, Wynn didn't think Lieutenant Stubbing would find anything. All of the staff had been at Stanford House for years, so they couldn't be accused. After that, the entire *belle monde* might as well be on the suspect list. Between his mother's cronies and his sister's cadre, the house was never empty, never secure from strangers. Just the night before Susan had held an impromptu ball, meaning she'd planned it for only weeks instead of months. Wynn hadn't known half the people drinking his champagne and eating his lobster patties, so he'd gone on to Maude's. He hadn't thought any of the guests even knew about the locked workshop next to his office. Stubbing was going over the guest list now, comparing the names to suspected traitors. He was also going to take over some of Wynn's escort duties so that his lordship could get to work on the replacement gifts for the generals' godsons.

Meanwhile, Viscount Stanford was pursuing his own inquiry, when he wasn't being besieged by one female or another. His mother had wheeled herself into his office as soon as he returned from Whitehall, and he had steeled himself for another lecture on late nights, loose women, and what was owed his lineage. Instead the dowager had been in a dither that one of the guests' hat had also disappeared last evening. Her favorite cisisbeo, Theodore, Lord Hume, could not find his top hat when he left the ball after the other guests had departed. Wynn didn't ask what Old Humidor was doing at Stanford House so late, because he didn't want to know. He did ask, "What is the big catastrophe, Mother? Most likely some other gentleman went home with Old Humi—ah, Lord Hume's topper."

"Well, they didn't, for there were no hats left, which there would have been if it was a simple mix-up."

"So someone forgot he came without a hat. It's no great mystery, Mother. The fellow will realize his error this morning"—as soon as he got a whiff of Hume's pervasive cigar smoke—"and return the thing. I trust Lord Hume's initials are inside."

Lady Stanford fidgeted with the handkerchief in her hand. "Yes, but that's not all."

Wynn could have sworn his mother's cheeks were flushed. "It's not?" he asked reluctantly, wishing he were in his workroom, shutting out petticoat problems.

The dowager stared at the cloth in her hands, avoiding her son's scrutiny. "You see, Theo kept something very dear to him in the lining of his hat."

"What kind of cocklehead keeps his treasures in the lining of his hat?" Wynn asked impatiently, one eye on the door to his workroom.

His mother snapped back, "The same kind of cocklehead who plays with toy soldiers."

Lady Stanford should have been working at the War Office.

"Yes, well, I'll check into it, Mother, and I'll tell Wilkins to be on the lookout. Now I really am quite busy."

Wynn would have discounted his mother's botheration as peculiar but not unusual except for the loss of his soldiers, which would have fit handily and unobtrusively in Old Humidor's hat, without making a bulge in someone's tailored coat. The tobacco stench might have peeled the paint off the castings, but no one would have noticed anything untoward.

But Wilkins would not have given Lord Hume's hat to just anyone. When asked, the butler did not recall an odd request or a guest straying to the cloakroom. And he always, Wilkins declared with stiffened spine, checked the initials inside every hat.

As soon as Stubbing completed his examination of the guest list, Wynn was going to go over it, matching initials. Then he'd pay a few calls just to make sure Tripp Hayes or Townsend Haverhill didn't have Theo Hume's chapeau by mistake. Haverhill had attended Susan's party in hopes of foisting his shrewish daughter off on Wynn, but the baron wouldn't get any false encouragement if Wynn bumped into him by chance at White's. Haverhill was known to spend most of his days— and nights—at White's, for which no one could blame him, so Wynn could avoid any potentially risky encounters. That rakehell Hadfield had been at Stanford House last evening, too, and Tully's pockets were perpetually to let, but insolvency didn't automatically make a man a thief or a traitor. There might be others with the initials; he'd have to check. And what the devil could Theo Hume be carrying in his hatband that had his mother in a fidge?

Deuce take it, when was he going to have time to work on his painting?

No time soon, it appeared, for the viscount's sister was next to arrive at his erstwhile private office. One look at her and Wynn's heart sank. Susan's face was red, her eyes were swollen, and she clutched a sodden handkerchief in one hand, a crumpled piece of paper in the other. Sarah Siddons before noon. Just what he needed.

"No."

Susan stopped short in midsob. "No? But I haven't said anything yet."

"No anyway. No whatever. No. No matter what it is you are hoping to wheedle out of me with your histrionics. No. And if you throw something else at me, Sukey, I swear I'll marry you off to the next man I see."

Stubbing coughed and backed out of the open door, red-faced.

Susan's gaze followed the officer's ramrod-straight back. "Who was that, Wynn?"

He groaned at the sudden interest in her voice. "My new secretary. No one for you to know. Now, please, Susan, I am busy. . . ."

"But, Wynn, we have to do something." She waved the paper in his face. "Miss Lockharte is dying! She might even be dead by now."

"Lockharte, is it? I couldn't tell. I got one of her missives also. High melodrama to make herself interesting, puss, nothing to send you into a decline."

"Oh, no, Wynn. There really is an epidemic at Miss Merrihew's. Most of the girls have been sent home. And Lady Mary did die. It was in the newspapers this morning. So, you see, you have to go to Brighton."

"*I* have to? She's your friend, Susan. Why aren't you going?"

"The Farragut rout is tonight and Almack's is tomorrow, then there is a theater party on Thursday. Besides, you'd never let me traipse off to Brighton by myself."

"True, but why the deuce should either of us be going to Brighton in the first place?"

"To help Miss Lockharte, noddy. I told you."

"I appreciate your confidence, puss, but if your friend is already dead, I'm afraid she's beyond even my help. I'm only a viscount, you know, not God."

"I know that you are being purposefully dense. You have to go to Miss Merrihew's at Worthing, outside Brighton, to make sure, to offer aid if need be, and to lay flowers on her grave."

"Good grief, why should I do any such thing? I never met the woman."

"Yes, you did. And you—we—did her a Great Wrong."

Wynn could hear the capital letters. He sighed for his lost morning, sure Susan was about to elucidate.

She dabbed at her eyes with the handkerchief. "I wanted her as my companion when I left Miss Merrihew's, but you said no."

Wynn vaguely recalled something of that nature, but he brushed it off. "You knew Cousin Lenore was coming. She's the perfect companion, up to every rig and row, widowed and respectable. And she needed the position."

"But Lenore is old, and Rosellen was my friend."

Lenore was Wynn's own age. He shrugged. "I am sure your friend found another post."

"That's the problem. She never did. Miss Merrihew wouldn't give her any references once she had given notice. Then the old witch was horrid to her, and now she's dead, and it's your fault. The least you can do is lay some flowers on her resting place. That was her last request."

Wynn seemed to recall that the termagant's last request was for his head on a platter. He rustled through the trash until he found her letter. He reread what he could of the splotched, crumpled mess. "It's no wonder she couldn't find another place teaching penmanship," he muttered.

Susan didn't wait for him to finish reading. "And she told me I had to be firm, I had to stand up for myself and not let you control my life with your high-handed ways."

"And you think I should have hired some . . . some seditionist to encourage you in this fustian, thinking you know better than your guardians?"

"It's not fustian, it's my future. And I will not marry your friend, no matter how many times you invite him for dinner. Doesn't the man have a cook of his own? For sure he doesn't have any conversation."

"Lenore has no trouble talking to Tripp Hayes."

"Then let Cousin Lenore marry the dullard. I will not." She stamped her foot for emphasis. "But that's not the point. Miss Lockharte encouraged me to learn resolution, to stand up for what I believe. I believe we owe her a decent burial, so what are you going to do about Miss Lockharte?"

"If she's dead, puss, there is nothing to be done. And if she's alive, there's no need to do anything."

"But Miss Merrihew is cruel."

And no other school would have an opening for a heretical, hysterical harridan with slovenly handwriting and a sharp tongue who wrote goosish letters. "Life can be cruel, puss."

Then Susan was in his arms, weeping. "But she was my friend, Wynn. She cared about me and my happiness, not just about money and titles."

Wynn patted her shoulder awkwardly. "I'm a trifle busy, puss, but I'll think about what we can do."

She sniffed. Then she sniffed again and stepped back. "You mean you're too busy with your ladybirds to help an honest lady."

"Dash it, what do you know of ladybirds, Sukey?"

"I know that Mama said you stank of cheap perfume, and she was right."

"She was wrong, my dear. It was very expensive perfume."

Chapter Five

$\mathcal{S}$ometimes the post brought glad tidings at Miss Merrihew's Select Academy for Young Females of Distinction: inquiries about new enrollments, cheques of deposit for current students. This was not one of those times.

"What are we going to do, Mirabel? The bitch seems to know everything. We have to get rid of her."

Miss Merrihew tore her letter in half, then half again and again until the pieces of her own expensive writing paper were smaller than her narrow, beady eyes, smaller than her sense of charity toward the letter's author. The paper was costly, but not nearly as costly as the wench's words would be, if made public. If the sanctimonious little scold told anyone about the rancid meats, the unqualified instructors, the pin money gone astray, to say nothing of the roving-eyed reverend, Mirabel Merrihew could move to the antipodes, for all the wealthy, well-born chits she'd be schooling.

She tossed the bits of paper into the flames of her sitting room's fireplace, the only fire kept constantly burning at the school. Then she held her bony fingers out for her companion's letter. "We'll get rid of her, all right, one way or t'other."

* * *

Sometimes the mail was early, sometimes the mail was late. And sometimes the Royal Mail was a trifle too diligent.

"Vivian, my love, this rather sad excuse for a letter has traveled after us from Bath to Bristol and back again. It is addressed to you, my precious."

Lady Comfrey, *née* Vivian Baldour, took the letter from her husband's hand, exchanging their squalling son for the penciled post. The earl jiggled the infant and cooed at him while his wife read. The babe stopped screaming and cooed back.

"Comfy, dear," Vivian said, looking up, "I think we are being blackmailed."

Lord Comfrey was holding his son, the son he never thought to have. The boy was surely the sturdiest, smartest infant in all of England. If the lad wasn't the handsomest, he soon would be, taking after his beautiful mother. Nothing could mar the earl's pleasure in this moment. "Ignore it, my love. That's the best way of dealing with such nuisances."

"But it's a tiresome letter from my old school, Comfy."

"I still say ignore it, precious. That Merrihew chap won't open his mouth, not if he knows what's good for him, and that old stick of a sister of his surely won't cry rope on you. Her school would suffer the same exposure. More, for you are a countess and she is a cit putting on airs."

"No, the letter is from one of the schoolteachers, Miss Lockharte. I recall that she was pleasant enough, if somewhat starchy."

"So what does she have to say for herself?"

"That she is dying, without ever having a child of her own."

"Well, I can see how that would be distressing, my love, but I don't think your correspondent intended it as a threat."

"You don't think it's a hint that she knows about little Algernon and means to tell everyone? I shouldn't like any more talk, Comfy." The gossipmongers had been working overtime when Vivian married the aged earl by special license; she did not want another breath of scandal. She liked her position as the eminently respectable and indulged darling of Bath society. The Reverend Mr. Merrihew, in fact, had done her the biggest favor of her life, the cad.

The earl handed his son over to the wet nurse, then came to stand behind his wife's shoulder. He put on his spectacles to read. "See, she wishes you happiness in your marriage, my love. I wouldn't worry. Send the female fifty pounds and be done with it."

"What if she really is dead?"

"Then she can't tell anyone about Algernon, can she?"

Letters? Litter, more like. Invites to places he didn't want to go, bills for purchases he hadn't wanted to make, that's all the post ever brought Lord Haverhill. Now this.

"Aggravation, aggravation, aggravation," he mumbled into his morning ale. Even his mistress was getting headaches. "Jamison," the baron bellowed for his butler. "Get my wife and daughter down here on the instant."

"But, my lord, it is not yet noon."

"And half of England has put in an honest day's work." Not Townsend Haverhill's half, of course, but someone was busy about delivering the post. Blast it to Hell!

Lady Haverhill fluttered into the breakfast room, took one look at her husband's clenched jaw, empurpled cheeks, and empty mug of ale, and backed out of the morning-room door, trailing scarves and shawls.

"Madam, you will do me the courtesy of attending me this morning."

The baroness nodded, shrank into her seat at the opposite end of the table, and reached for her smelling salts.

"My word, woman, I am not about to carve you up for breakfast!" he shouted, making the baroness cringe deeper into her chair.

Thunderation, Lord Haverhill swore to himself, his wife was a rabbit and his daughter was a vixen, which made him a jackass.

Clarice wasn't half pleased to be rousted out of her room

before she was entirely satisfied with her ensemble for the day. "What is the problem, Papa? You know I don't like to be disturbed, especially when I'm not ready for morning callers."

"Morning callers be hanged. This"—he waved a letter in the air with the hand not holding his mug out to be refilled—"is the problem. This morning I received a farewell message from my niece at that school, saying she is sick and likely to die."

Lady Haverhill gasped and clutched her vinaigrette, while Jamison finished pouring, then beat a hasty retreat, shutting the door behind him, but Clarice merely reached for a slice of toast. "Fiddle. Rosellen always took herself too seriously, Papa. I received a note from her, too, and you may rest assured that I paid it no nevermind."

"I should rest comfortably knowing that you don't care if your only cousin might be sticking her spoon in the wall?"

Clarice paused in buttering her bread to look at her father with wide blue eyes. "Why ever should it matter? It's not as if I have to go into black gloves or anything."

"Good grief, the chit is your own kin."

"But it's not as though we were close. I never saw her in my life until that Season she embarrassed us all with her turnip manners. You were the one who declared the Lockhartes beneath us for all those years, Father, you know you were, so you cannot fault me now. I don't recall hearing any remorse when Rosellen's mother died."

The baron gnashed his teeth. The chit had a point, one he was not proud of, but a point nonetheless. "My sister was married. She was the vicar's responsibility. Rosellen is mine. She may be dying, and we may be accountable for her demise."

Clarice gave a trill of laughter, a sound she was practicing for effect. Now that she wasn't a debutante, titters just wouldn't do; she needed trills. "Oh, Father, how you go on. We haven't seen hide nor hair of the farouche female in two years. I'm sure noble houses cannot be expected to keep track of every ragtag twig on the family tree."

"I sent my sister's only child to that school you attended because you said she was ruined."

His wife spoke up now. "She was on the terrace with that dreadful Dawe boy. Everyone saw her, Townsend. We really could not have kept such a wanton under our roof. Why, there might have been a scandal."

"There *was* a scandal, madam, for which I blamed Rosellen. Now I am not so certain. I always thought there was something havey-cavey about that night, the vicar's daughter going off with a known rake."

"I saw her myself, Father, in his embrace."

The baron tapped the letter with his fork. "And looks can be deceiving, missy, as I know to my sorrow." There was his beautiful daughter, looking like butter wouldn't melt in her mouth, and she had the soul of a Billingsgate fishwife.

"I'm sure I don't know what you mean, Father."

Perhaps she didn't. "Rosellen told me not to judge so hastily, Clarice, so we'll discuss it again after we've seen her, if it's not too late."

"What do you mean, 'after we've seen her'? Surely you are not bringing that impossible female back here? A schoolteacher, Father? Shall you try to get your valet into White's next?" Clarice practiced her trill again.

"My niece is a schoolteacher because I condemned her without a hearing, missy, on your say-so. I sent her to Miss Merrihew's also on your say-so, where she has been cheated and mistreated, possibly mortally affected. If nothing else, we owe her a decent burial. She wants to be placed with her parents in St. Jerome parish."

Clarice jumped to her feet, overturning her chair and the teapot that was at her elbow. Her blue eyes were mere slits and her rose-tinged cheeks were splotched with angry red circles. If any of her suitors could see her now, her father reflected, they'd head for the hills faster than a poacher with a brace of partridges. One look at her daughter's face and Lady Haverhill crawled under the table, pretending to mop at the spill with her lace-edged handkerchief.

Clarice pounded on the mahogany. "I am not going into mourning for some nobody just because you've suffered an attack of conscience. You could have forced Rolly Dawe to marry her before he rejoined his regiment, or you could have given her a dowry to make her undistinguished birth more palatable to some other barely eligible *parti*. But all you did was foist the parson's brat off on me. My clothes, my friends, my connections. She was *my* cross to bear. I got rid of her then and I am not having her back, ruining another Season, dead or alive."

"Clarice," her mother wheezed from under the table while Baron Haverhill reached for the brandy decanter on the sideboard.

Clarice wasn't finished. "Furthermore, I refuse to go into half-mourning for your suddenly precious niece, because I look peaked in lavender, and I absolutely will not retire to the country during the height of the Season, especially when I am about to bring Stanford up to scratch."

Lord Haverhill choked on his drink, and not just because it was too early in the day for such strong spirits or strong emotions. "Stanford? You've been chasing the poor devil for two years and haven't gotten an inch closer to him. The man didn't even stay to dance with you at his own sister's party last night."

Clarice raised her chin. "He told me I was in looks."

"You're always in looks, missy, when you're out in public. So is his bird of paradise, and he ain't going to marry Maude Jenkins either."

Lady Stanford was lying on the carpet now, gasping like a grunion on the beach. Her husband and daughter glared at each other, ignoring her.

"I'll have you know that Viscount Stanford paid me particular attention last night before he left. He made a point of telling me he regretted that he could not stay at the dance since he had another engagement. I expect him to be paying you a call any day now."

"And I expect Farmer George to show up in his nightshirt. Stanford has nice manners, that's all, you widgeon. Just because a chap is polite don't mean he's ready to drop the handkerchief. Stanford is too downy a cove to be taken in by a pretty face, girl, and the sooner you realize that, the sooner you might try prettying up your disposition."

"Now you sound just like that mealymouthed Rosellen, telling me I should improve my mind. Hah! My mind's not the one writing sermons to virtual strangers. I'm not languishing at a girls' school or trying to weasel my way back into favor."

"No, you're just making a permanent place for yourself on the shelf. If you spent half as much time improving your character as you do improving your wardrobe, I might get you off my hands at last."

Now Clarice gasped. Her father had never spoken to her that way. "Father!"

"Well, it's true. A man don't want a woman cutting up his peace all the time." He looked over the edge of the table at his prostrate wife. "And the plain and simple truth is that you're selfish and spoiled, missy. Saw it m'self, but it was too late to bolt the barn door after the mare was gone. And I let you destroy a young woman's entire life."

"Rosellen Lockharte was born to be a schoolteacher. She was raised a poor bluestocking in a backwater borough. If she dies the way she lived, it is no fault of mine. Now I pray you'll excuse me. I have to get ready for morning callers."

"And I have to go bury my niece."

the brothers made themselves comfortable on the only two

Chapter Six

*N*o one ever wrote to the Heatherstone twins. Why bother? Bills never got paid, invitations never got acknowledged, correspondence never got found in the rats' nest the two brothers shared at the Albany. No one knew if the two chuckleheads could read. Instead, merchants dispatched their accountings to Sir Harry, their long-suffering father, who stayed a long way away. Hostesses sent footmen to find out if the twins meant to attend their dinners or card parties, and acquaintances simply tracked them down in the park, at the latest mill, or at the feet of the reigning Incomparable. Two carrot-topped Tulips were easy to locate.

Chance alone put a letter into each of the brothers' hands, Chance being the name of the porter who was sorting the post that morning at the exact moment the twins were returning to their apartment after a night of carousing. Timothy and Thomas made their unsteady way up the stairs, then tossed their high, starched cravats and tightly fitting, wasp-waisted coats onto the already tall piles on the floor, tables, and chairs of their sitting room. They pulled off each other's boots, then Tim found two halfway clean glasses while Tom searched for the flint to light the fire. Finally, brandies in one hand, letters in the other, the brothers made themselves comfortable on the only uncluttered surfaces, matching worn leather armchairs.

Tim held his letter up to his nose and sniffed. "Not a high flyer."

Tom turned his over and studied the crude candlewax seal. "Not a lady."

Common belief had it that twins could read each other's thoughts. Luckily, the Heatherstones had little in the way of thoughts, for they read minds as easily as they read letters. Still, they managed to communicate as well as any two heads of cabbage. As one, they opened the letters. The fire crackled, lips mumbled the words. Then, silently, they traded letters. The fire crackled, lips mumbled the same words again.

They looked up at the same time, three shades paler. The drained color revealed that Timothy, the elder, had approximately fifteen more freckles than Thomas, the younger by twenty minutes. Timothy was the first to speak. "What do you think?"

"I didn't know ladies liked dogs."

"Not that part. Do you think we did it?"

"We never said she couldn't have a dog."

"Forget about the dog; did we ruin a gentlewoman?"

A minute went by while Tom deliberated. "We were only doing what Clarice Haverhill asked us to do, and trying to help her win that bet with Tully, of course. Didn't think anything would come of it. We lost, besides."

"Beautiful gel. First class."

It did not take any supernatural powers of communication for Tom to understand that his brother wasn't referring to Miss Haverhill's dowdy, commonplace country cousin. "Rich, too."

"I thought she'd have one of us if we made the wager for her."

"Deuced lucky thing she didn't."

"Bitch."

"First class."

Together they stared into the fire, sipping their brandies.

"It was Rolly Dawe who kissed her," Tom said after a bit.

Tim nodded. "And now he's dead. Do you think she did it?"

"Took a French bullet. That's what they said at the Cocoa Tree."

"But she said she'd get even. And I lost a monkey tonight."

"And I had a nightmare yesterday. Dreamt I was hitched to Mrs. Fitzherbert."

They both shuddered and drained their glasses. "Lud, maybe the female is already haunting us, a warning-like. She said she wouldn't rest easy."

The freckles stood out like inkblots on both faces. "Maybe she ain't dead," Tim suggested hopefully.

His brother was eager to agree. "Ghosts can't have revenge if they ain't dead, can they?"

Tim sagely pronounced, "If they ain't dead, they ain't ghosts."

"Good thinking, bro. So what should we do?"

"Better find out."

Tom was still troubled by visions of Prinny's old mistress. "But if she is dead, what should we do? We ought to have a plan."

"Leave the country, maybe."

"Spirits don't travel? I never knew that. The pater don't like to leave Yorkshire, but I didn't think spooks were so finicky."

"No, I mean we could join the army. The female says we better not dishonor another lady. No ladies in Spain."

"No? What do Spanish gentlemen do?"

Tim frowned at his brother. "Dash it, pay attention. If we stole her honor, maybe we can make up for it in the army. For God, king, and country, don't you know?"

"Always admired the uniforms. But the pater won't like it."

"He don't like rackety ways either. The governor will be happy to see the last of us. He's always saying we're worthless fribbles, ain't he? He swears we'll never amount to anything, every chance he gets, don't he?"

"We could amount to cannon fodder. We don't have to die so Miss Lockharte don't haunt us, do we?"

"War's almost over. No chance of that."

"That's all right then," Tom said.

"It's all right," Tim said, "unless the female ain't dead. What do we do then?"

"We buy her a dog?"

"That ain't going to give her back what we stole."

"We weren't the ones who stole that kiss, remember? It was old Rolly, by George. Thought we were clear on that."

"Dash it, Tom, we stole her reputation, just like she said in the letter. Gentlemen don't ruin ladies," he declared, maintaining his twenty-minute maturity. "We've got to do right by her. You'll marry her."

Tom almost fell off his chair. "Me? Why not you? You're the older. The one who is going to be baronet someday. More honor in that than marrying a plain mister. Ladies like titles, don't you know."

"But they don't like living in a cottage, which is all either of us could afford. You know the governor said we're too expensive for a poor female, so one of us has to marry money. Rich chits are more likely to fall in the heir's lap than the spare's."

Tom shoved an unmatched glove, a half-eaten roll, and a stack of racing forms off the table beside his chair. Under it all he came up with a deck of cards. "We'll play for it."

Tim wasn't so sure. "Winner gets the girl?"

"Hell, no. Winner gets to join the army. Loser gets the leg-shackles."

"Uh, maybe we better let the woman pick—if she ain't dead. Better go find her at that place in Worthing. Save her life, what?"

"Regular heroes, that's us. So do we ride or drive?"

"Now how are we going to bring a sickly female away from some academy on horseback? You ain't thinking, Tom."

"Seems to me we've done more thinking now than in the

last five years. Giving me the headache, it is. So we'll drive. My curricle or yours?"

"My bays are faster than your nags."

"Are not. Your slugs will be winded before we've gone ten miles."

"We'll race."

Tom wasn't so sure. "What's the winner get?"

"He gets to Worthing first, you clunch."

"Uh, Tim, where is Worthing?"

"Damned if I know."

Viscount Stanford hadn't placed the Heatherstone twins on his mental list of suspects for either stealing his soldiers or making off with Hume's hat. He hadn't recalled their first names or initials, since he always thought of them merely as Rattle and Pate. But he did remember that they'd been at his house the night before once he saw their names on the guest list Stubbing had compiled with the butler's help. They'd been wearing yellow Cossack trousers and puce waistcoats with cabbage roses embroidered on them. With their red hair, Haddock and Hake had looked like wallpaper for a whorehouse. And they'd been making calf's eyes at Susan. The Heatherstones were known to follow the latest fashions, both in their attire and in paying court to the latest belle. Wynn was pleased that his sister had the nod, but not from those noddies, as rackety a pair as he'd ever known. They'd always seemed harmless enough, but someone had been in his studio.

Wynn's first call, after discussing the list with Stubbing, was at the Albany. The porter there reported that the twins had left in tandem an hour earlier, arguing over horses, roads, and who would pay the tolls.

"I wouldn't be surprised if they came a-cropper before they reach Reigate, the way they was carrying on." The porter was garrulous, with a new guinea in his pocket. "On the go and on the wrong road for Brighton."

They were cow-handed, to boot. But what the deuce were those two jackstraws doing, going to Brighton?

"Trying to beat Prinny's time, from what I heard," the porter said, shaking his head at the young men's chances.

"But during the Season?" Wynn wondered out loud. "Those two nodcocks never miss a free meal."

The porter had no answer. "Maybe they don't know it ain't summer yet."

"Do you mind if I go up and leave a message?"

For another guinea, the porter wouldn't have minded if Viscount Stanford left the twins a mangel-wurzel. "You can try, but they'll never find it in that pigsty."

Wynn looked around the sitting room, not even pretending to be seeking a safe place for his calling card. Lud, his pigs lived better than this.

"The maids come on Thursdays. They do the best they can, but it would take more'n a dustmop and a broom to make this place look presentable."

A fire or an earthquake, perhaps, Wynn thought. He did find a top hat, resting on a bust of Homer that could only have come with the furnished rooms. He smelled the hat while the porter shrugged at the ways of the gentry.

"Queer as Dick's hatband, all of 'em," he muttered.

No, there was nothing in the hatband or the lining either, just the stamped initials TH. And the hat smelled of London's stews, not of cigar smoke. Wynn gave up the search. A battalion of his miniature soldiers could have bivouacked in this dump and he wouldn't spot them. So he left, stepping on the letters that had sent the Heatherstones hying for the high road.

The rooms belonging to Tripp Hayes, the Honorable Thorence Hayes the Third, that was, were ascetic in contrast. Nothing was out of place or less than immaculate, including Tripp's valet, Fullerton. The fastidious gentleman's gentleman was packing.

"Mr. Hayes has decided to visit his family," the gray-clad

servant said with a sniff, expressing his opinion of gentlemen who went haring around the countryside without their valets. "Quite unexpectedly. I shall follow this afternoon with the baggage."

"Nothing wrong with his mother, I trust."

"I'm sure I couldn't say, not being in the master's confidence." Which the little man obviously resented.

He also couldn't say when Hayes might be returning to Town. He was, however, able to state unequivocally that no hats had suffered mistaken identity at his hands. "Ours are made by Locke, of course."

"Yes, but Locke makes a great many hats and some have the same initials."

The valet drew himself up to his full height, nose twitching. "Mr. Hayes has never and would never put on another gentleman's hat."

And he would never betray his country or his friends, Wynn was willing to swear. He'd be the perfect match for his peagoose of a sister, if only she could be made to see Tripp's sterling qualities. The only thing that nagged at the viscount—and it truly was a small thing, he told himself—was that Tripp's mother lived in Bognor Regis, along the southern coast where smugglers were known to ply their trade with France. It was also along the same coast as Brighton, as a matter of fact.

Tully Hadfield wasn't at home at the run-down rooming house where he boarded. Seeing a squad of bailiffs at the door, Wynn was not surprised Hadfield had done a flit, but he was not happy either to see that the rake was in such dire straits. Punting on tick, a man could grow desperate.

Wynn checked the stable where he knew Hadfield kept his cattle. As he'd expected, they were missing, too. The ostler hadn't seen Tully leave, else he would have called for the bailiffs himself. Now he'd never be paid. Wynn tossed him a coin for his troubles. Blast, there'd be no finding Tully's direction now. He could be halfway to France with Wynn's handiwork and Old Humidor's hat.

Wynn's last stop was at White's, in search of Townsend Haverhill. To the doorman's surprise, the baron hadn't been in yet today. Lud, the viscount did not want to call at the baron's house. He might as well put his head in the lion's mouth as pay a call on Clarice Haverhill. The baron was his last chance of recovering Lord Hume's hat, though, with whatever secrets it contained.

Fortunately, he did not have to go into Haverhill House. In the doorway he asked the butler if he might speak with the baron.

"Milord is not in, Lord Stanford. May I take your card up to the ladies?" He held out a white-gloved hand for the ritual calling card, one corner turned down to show that the viscount had called in person. The butler would carry it up the stairs, ask his mistress if she was receiving, then stand back lest he be trampled in Miss Clarice's eagerness to snag the eminently eligible lord. Wagers among the footmen were two to one in Miss Clarice's favor.

Wynn placed a pound note on the butler's palm instead. "Forget I even stopped by, will you?"

The butler noted that his lordship wasn't carrying a nosegay or a box of bonbons. There was no ring-box-size bulge in the coat stretched across a broad chest. Jamison nodded. He'd back the winner, and Miss Clarice could lead apes in hell. The pound note disappeared discreetly.

Wynn had a second one ready. "Perhaps you could tell me where I might find Baron Haverhill? Another of my guests last evening mislaid a personal item and I was wondering if the baron had seen it."

Jamison eyed the paper money with regret. "I am sorry, my lord, but Baron Haverhill has gone out of town on a family matter. He expects to return from Worthing within a sennight."

Worthing, on the seacoast between Brighton and Bognor

Regis? The same Worthing where Wynn's sister had gone to school, where that female was dead or dying? Impossible! Ridiculous! Out of the question.

Dash it, Wynn swore as he made his way back to Grosvenor Square, he might have to call on Miss Lockharte after all.

Chapter Seven

*W*hen the viscount returned to Stanford House, he handed Wilkins his hat and gloves. The butler handed him more headaches.

"Mr. Stubbing asked to be notified immediately at your arrival, my lord. He is in the office. Lady Stanford requests you attend her in her chamber, and Miss Susan is waiting for you in the morning room. Also Lord Hume has called. I put him in the library."

"What, Cousin Lenore doesn't want to talk to me?"

"I regret to say that Mrs. Dahlquist is ailing. She has not come out of her room today."

"Has the doctor been called?"

"No, my lord. The note from under Mrs. Dahlquist's door requested that she be permitted to rest today, that there was nothing terribly wrong."

"Most likely she was sick and tired of Susan's pleas to attend the masquerade. With that rake Hadfield out of town, maybe we'll get some peace."

"Yes, my lord."

Wynn stood in the hall, brushing his dark hair back with his fingers, trying to decide where he ought to go first, other than back to White's.

"And this was delivered while you were out, my lord."

On a silver tray that usually held invitations and calling cards reposed the remains of a miniature of himself that Maude had commissioned, at his expense, of course. The frame had been smashed, the painting sliced. Maude was nothing if not thorough.

"It does not appear to have been a very good likeness, my lord," the butler commiserated.

"*Au contraire, mon ami,* it is a perfect representation of how I am feeling: battered and torn, ready for the dust heap."

"Perhaps Mrs. Dahlquist's ailment is contagious."

"Ah, but I can neither take to my bed nor hide under the covers, can I?" Then again, if he'd stayed at Maude's, in her bed, he wouldn't have had an expensive trinket in smithereens, or his peace entirely cut up.

The butler did not bother answering; he merely informed the viscount that Lady Stanford seemed quite perturbed, as did Miss Susan and Lord Hume.

"Right, I'll check in with Stubbing first then."

"Excellent, my lord. I'll bring the brandy directly."

"That bad, eh? I don't suppose any odd hats have been returned?"

The butler just shook his head in regret and sympathy.

Stubbing hadn't found any clues to the missing soldiers either. None of the guests was on Whitehall's suspect list or Bow Street's thief-takers' roster. A few of the nobs, like Lord Hadfield, were known to be below hatches.

"I am not disparaging the ruling class, my lord, my own father being one of them, but it's the truth that men living beyond their means cannot always be trusted." The men were sitting at either side of Wynn's wide desk, the cut-crystal decanter between them.

Wynn swirled the brandy in his glass and agreed. "At least

you're honest. If we consider everyone punting on tick to be a traitor, though, we might as well hang half of Parliament."

The officer nodded, then continued: "We are not hopeful, although our people are watching the usual scoundrels."

"No, my people are too small, too easily hidden or disguised as children's playthings."

"Precisely what made them so valuable to us in the past. I am afraid we shall have to discontinue the operation for now. General's orders."

"No more lead soldiers?" Wynn tried to keep the disappointment from his voice. Dash it, he'd been doing something worthwhile.

"The general says that you should keep painting, in case. He's hopeful the war will be ended shortly anyway, but then you can give them to your sons."

"I don't have any sons."

Stubbing looked down at the papers in his hands. "The general mentioned that, too. He seems to feel it is the responsibility of the nobility to provide for the future."

"Blast him for an interfering old busybody then."

Stubbing cleared his throat, sudden color coming to his fair cheeks. "The general is my godfather, my lord."

"My apologies, Lieutenant, but I get enough of such lectures from my mother."

"I understand, my lord, and there are times when I do appreciate being a second son. No one is concerned with the proliferation of more cadets."

"And you got to join up."

The lieutenant tapped his stiff leg. "Not always a blessing."

"Sorry, that was thoughtless of me. But tell me, Lieutenant, are you being recalled to Whitehall or can you stay on a few days? I have an idea or two about the missing soldiers. There have been some odd coincidences lately."

The young man smiled his pleasure at being invited to stay. Stanford House was decidedly an improvement on the army barracks. "Rare things, coincidences," he said, sipping his smooth, well-aged drink.

"That's what I thought."

When his discussion with Stubbing was over, Wynn went upstairs to scratch on his mother's door. He hadn't had enough to drink to face telling his sister that her would-be paramour would be imprisoned for debt if he showed his face again. And Old Humidor was his mother's problem, not his.

"No, I cannot face him," she cried from her chaise longue, having stuffed the novel she was reading under the cushions. Fluttering her handkerchief, she moaned weakly. "It is all my fault, and now we'll be ruined. Susan will never make a good marriage, my only son will hate me forever, and dear Theo will be banned from his clubs."

"Good grief, Mother, what did the two of you do that you confessed in a hatband? No, please don't tell me, I beg of you. And please do not get yourself in such a state. It isn't good for your health. No one is going to broadcast your secrets, and if they do, no one is going to give the gossip any credit. You are a viscountess, for heaven's sake, one of the doyennes of the *haut monde*. Now why don't we go down and let Old, ah, Lord Hume take you for a ride in the park?"

"No, I cannot go out. I cannot face the world." The hand at her breast added a nice, dramatic touch, she thought.

It also dislodged the novel, which fell at Wynn's feet. He eyed her suspiciously. "Coming too strong, *maman*. Just what is it that you don't want to do?"

The dowager straightened the blanket on her knees, not looking at her handsome, cynical son. She didn't even try to gammon him anymore. "Lenore is sick and cannot chaperon your sister tonight."

"Do not look at me that way, Mother. It won't kill the chit to stay home for once. She can spend one evening reading improving works or doing needlework with you. It seems to me that you've been embroidering the same chair cushions for the last six years."

Lady Stanford did not want to discuss her embroidery or the purple-covered novels residing in her workbasket. "Your sister is a debutante. She must go out, must be seen."

He snorted. "She's been out for well over a year, Mother, and is an acclaimed Toast. She is hardly liable to be forgotten in one night."

"She has already accepted."

"Then you and Hume can take her to whichever ball or breakfast or whatever the boring entertainment is tonight."

"Theo is too distressed. He really is, Wynn. And he gets dyspeptic when he is upset. Besides, he hates to play for the chicken stakes at those affairs."

"I see, so you think to foist the escort duty off on me. It won't wash, Mother. I have more important things to do."

"Like hide out in that smelly workroom? Or stay all night at that place in Kensington?"

"What do you know about the place in Kensington?"

"What, do you think your father didn't have his *chère amie* stashed somewhere, that I wouldn't know about such things? If he hadn't, Theo and I mightn't have—but that's not the point. You should be going to these affairs, Wynn, to find a wife. Just think, then it would be *her* duty to chaperon your sister."

"Zeus, how did we get from Hume's heartburn to my bride? You haven't been talking to the chaps at Whitehall, have you?"

"Well, Susan is not going to find an eligible *parti* sitting at home either. I'll never have grandchildren at this rate."

"Mother, I—"

"Go. What do you care that I should be back in Bath, where the doctors are knowledgeable about my condition, the waters are healthful, and the air is clean? You're too selfish to get married, and now you won't help your sister find a husband."

What, did his mother think he wanted her and Susan living in his house forever? The viscount had been trying to get the chit fired off for ages, it seemed. He might have more luck if she stopped weeping.

"Dash it, Sukey, you look like a sausage, all red and puffy. And I don't appreciate your turning into a watering pot over some foolish masquerade."

Susan left the window seat in the morning room, where she'd been staring out at the park across the way. "You really are a heartless beast, Wynn Alton. I'm not crying over missing a masked ball, although I have never been to one at Vauxhall because you are too stiff-rumped to take me. I am distressed, which you would understand if you had the least consideration for others' feelings, over the plight of poor Miss Lockharte. She was right, Wynn, you do show a callous disregard for those you consider beneath you, which is practically everyone."

" 'Heartless beast,' 'callous disregard'? Now why do those phrases sound familiar? Your penmanship instructor didn't write all that to you, too, did she?"

"Of course not. She wished me courage and happiness, as I told you. But that's what she wrote in her letter to you. And don't look daggers at me, Wynn. If you hadn't wanted me to see it, you shouldn't have left the letter lying around."

"It wasn't lying around, by George. It was in my desk in my office!"

"I needed some paper."

"You needed a better look at Stubbing, I suppose."

"You must admit he is attractive."

"I must admit nothing of the kind, Sukey, and neither must you. Stubbing is a mere second son with connections that might lead to a government post if he is lucky. He could never support you in the style you're used to, so don't think to set up one of your flirtations with him. He is not up to your weight."

"Now you are being hateful, and all because you know I'm right. You *are* arrogant and selfish, just as Miss Lockharte said."

"Dash it, stop quoting the deplorable female, brat. I don't need to hear one more word from her or you."

"She is not deplorable, sirrah; she is dying, of your cold-hearted neglect. Poor Miss Lockharte is most likely dead by now." Susan started weeping again at the thought.

Wynn was disgusted. "Overwrought and unbalanced, your friend might be. Dead, no. No one at death's door knocks so loudly. Her drivel contained so much contempt, so much scathing denunciation of the whole aristocracy, that she simply couldn't be ready to cash in her chips. Confound it, with instructors like that, it's no wonder you turned out to be a spoiled widgeon. I don't believe you care half as much for your sick schoolteacher as you pretend. You're upset because Lenore cannot take you to your party tonight."

"Well, you are far off the mark. Why should I be upset about missing Lady Carrington's musicale? Mama said you would escort me. You'll adore it. Lady Carrington's niece is going to play the harp."

Wynn could think of only one thing to do. He stood in the hall and shouted for Stubbing.

Lord Hume stuck his bald head out of the library door. "Ah, home, are you, Stanford? I've been wanting a word with you."

Wynn combed his hands through his already disordered curls and gnashed his teeth. "Yes, sir, I'll be right there. Just trying to arrange an escort for my sister to tonight's entertainment."

"Good," the earl said, heading back into the library. "I can't stand the deuced caterwauling myself. I told your mother you'd find a way to get out of it."

There was no way Wynn was going to get out of hearing Lord Hume's confession. Feet dragging, he followed the older man into his own bookroom, which was so thick with smoke that he could barely make out the shelves of books. He opened a window while Lord Hume lumbered over to the most comfortable chair in the room and lowered himself into it. "Smoke, my boy?" he offered, holding out a fresh cigar. The one in his other hand was a thick, sodden mess, with leaves coming unwrapped from being gnawed on. Wynn declined politely, then poured himself a glass of wine. He went to stand next to the window, not caring that the early spring day was dank and cold. He was never going to get back to his soldiers, at this rate.

"Bit of a pickle, what?" the antique aristocrat asked, his florid cheeks like bellows as he puffed away.

It was a devil of a coil, letting the army's secrets fall into enemy hands.

"I know it was foolish to have it lying around, but I liked to have the note near me."

Wynn realized the elderly earl was speaking of his blasted hat. "Couldn't you have kept it in your pocket?"

"M'valet goes through the pockets, don't you know. Couldn't trust the chap not to pocket it, like he does with m'loose change, or toss it in the trash."

"Then a safe? Wouldn't that have been the better place for such an incriminating, ah, important document?"

"Likely it would, but I thought it brought me luck all these years. You know what they say about unlucky in love, lucky at cards, or something like that. I felt like I had an angel on m'shoulder, don't you know."

Wynn thought he did. Old Humidor had never wed, not even with a title to pass down, although Wynn thought there were nephews in line for the earldom. But he'd been wearing the willow for all these years and a *billet-doux* next to his heart. Or next to his balding pate. The idea that this tobacco-stained knight of the baize table had loved a female all these years was so sweet, it was making the viscount ill. No, that was the cigar smoke.

"Thing is, the note would embarrass your dear mama."

"She wrote the letter, I suppose?" Wynn asked, resigned to the worst.

Hume spit out a mouthful of wet tobacco. "Said she loved me. I was honored."

"And I gather she signed the letter? And addressed it to you?"

The earl nodded.

"Well, I can't see what all the fuss is about. The ton knows you dote on my mother. Everyone is used to seeing you together, here and in Bath."

"She dated it."

Whoever thought women should be educated to read and write ought to be shot. Between that dreadful dying woman in Worthing and his own dear, dunderheaded mother, Wynn felt like tearing his hair out. Except then he might look like Theo Hume, combing his hair across his forehead, all six strands of it. The viscount had a more horrifying thought: Perhaps he was destined to look like the earl anyway. How did one ask one's own mother's paramour such a question? Pardon, Earl, but are you my papa? Hell and damnation. "I take it the date preceded my father's death?"

Hume blew a smoke ring, so he'd have something to stare at, rather than his host. "Loved her forever, it seems. But her father wanted Stanford's blunt for his gel. Arranged marriage, don't you know."

Wynn knew he wasn't getting an answer. He supposed it wasn't any of his business, except he might not be his father's heir. "Why the deuce don't you marry her now, then? You wouldn't have to worry about any gossip."

"I've asked once a month since your mother put off her blacks. First of the month, like clockwork. That way I won't forget. She won't have me till you and Susan are settled respectably. Then you can't be touched by any scandals from the past. Says it's her duty to Stanford."

No wonder she wanted to see him wed, and Susan, too, Wynn thought.

The earl was going on, talking around the stump of a cigar in his mouth. "She'll never have me, now that I've gone and put her family in danger of being ostracized from Polite Society. Susan most of all."

Wynn thought he knew the date on the letter now. "Perhaps it will never come to that. I still think someone took the hat in error. It could be returned any day."

The earl shook his head, his jowls flapping. "Lost my letter, lost my lady, lost my love." A tear wended its slow way down his ruddy cheek.

Wynn knew he had to do something to keep the family skeletons in the closet, where they belonged. He wasn't a careless care-for-naught, despite Miss Lockharte's opinion of his character. "I have a few leads to pursue," he told Lord Hume now, "gentlemen I haven't been able to question because they've gone out of Town. With you and Stubbing to keep an eye on things here, I might as well follow them all south."

That way, his library might have aired out by the time he got back, and he could hunt for his missing soldiers. And while he was in the vicinity, Wynn reluctantly conceded, he might as well look up his sister's mortally ill—or mentally unstable—mentor. Lud, he was actually going to Brighton.

Miss Rosellen Lockharte, meanwhile, was going to Heaven.

Chapter Eight

*H*eaven was just as Rosellen had imagined, all white and soft, downy and cushiony. The clouds were like pillows and she was melting into their gentle welcome. She couldn't see anything, or else her eyes would not open, but that was all right. She was content to drift in the fleece. Then a shadow seemed to cross over her and the surrounding billows shifted beneath her. Rosellen wondered if she'd have to share her cloud, the way she'd had to share her bed when she first came to Miss Merrihew's.

Rosellen was not quite as comfortable, not quite as secure on her cloud. She still couldn't see, but now she couldn't breathe either. Perhaps one was not supposed to need air in Heaven, but surely angels didn't go around gasping and wheezing for breath, as she seemed to be doing. What was the point of clouds if they covered one's nose and mouth? She'd have to ask her father about that. Surely he'd know. Meanwhile, she tried to pull the cloud away. Sticking plaster could not have adhered more firmly. She couldn't even call for help.

Suddenly there was less pressure on her face and Rosellen took a deep, revitalizing breath. She thought she heard Fanny say, "Here now, miss, how did you get yourself all tangled up like this? Tryin' to dance a hornpipe afore you got your sea legs back?"

"Fanny, you're an angel," Rosellen managed to say when she had enough air in her lungs. The little maid must have caught the influenza, too, poor thing. And no wonder, the way she'd been run ragged. Rosellen hoped she hadn't suffered long.

Bustling about at the bedside with a cup of broth, Fanny laughed. "And didn't the bloke at the receiving office say the same thing when he saw me in the red cloak."

"Oh, did you get a new mantle?"

"Still all about in your head, I see. Doctor says the fever's gone now; you just need to get your strength up. Best drink your broth and hurry recoverin'. Mistress won't be letting me wait on the likes of you once the payin' students come back."

This made no sense whatsoever to Rosellen, but she told herself she'd figure it out once she had a bit more rest. She started to drift away on her clouds again, thankfully on top of them rather than in their smothering midst.

"And all your letters got delivered," Fanny said, proud she'd managed the task without Miss Merrihew being any the wiser.

Letters? What letters?

Heaven had to take some getting used to. This time her robes seemed to be choking her, tightening around her neck. But then, right before she was about to lodge a complaint, there was Fanny, her personal angel. In a few minutes Rosellen could breathe, she could swallow, she could even speak a little.

"Are you finding things odd here, Fanny?" she asked.

"Only how you can't lift a hand to hold your spoon, but you manage to get all twisted up every time I turn my back. Brung you some nice porridge, I did, and a surprise."

Rosellen was finding enough surprises, thank you. Gruel, in

Heaven? Surely the heavenly host could manage better than that. She pushed the spoon away.

Fanny was too excited to notice. "A grand coach pulled up this morning, miss, and you'll never guess, but a liveried footman stepped out and asked for you! I thought Miss Merrihew would have a spasm, that he wasn't come about some wealthy new chit for the school. He insisted this come right into your hands, he did, so she let me bring it. You should've seen him, tall and handsome, with a white wig and dressed all in gold."

"That must have been Gabriel then. Not a wig. Did he have a horn?"

"What, to blow for the tolls? That'd be the coachman's job or the guard's. You ain't listenin', miss. I hope that fever didn't leave you dicked in the nob, 'cause I don't know what you keep blatherin' on about. Miss Merrihew won't be happy iffen you ain't fit to teach the young ladies next week. But here, see what the fellow brung you. He didn't wait for a reply, neither, so you can't send it back, whatever it is."

Fanny placed a small pouch on Rosellen's chest. She clucked her tongue when Miss Lockharte made no move to open the strings. "Lud, I'd have to be half-dead before I let the thing sit like that," she said impatiently.

All dead, Rosellen didn't care, still worrying over why Gabriel would let a coachman blow his trumpet.

Fanny took the pouch back and opened it herself. "Coo, miss, look at this! It's a regular fortune! Near fifty pounds, I swear! You're rich!"

Rosellen always thought you couldn't take wealth with you, not that she had any to take. Now she was in funds, and defunct. What a shame. "Too late," she murmured.

"Never too late to be lyin' in clover, that's what I say."

"Clouds, not clover." Though perhaps clover wouldn't be quite so difficult to tame as her cantankerous clouds.

"You sure found the silver linin' with those letters, miss."

"Letters?"

"Lud, don't you remember anything? You was feverish and

delirious, I s'pose, but you was determined to write those letters, iffen it took your last breath."

It must have.

Rosellen wasn't in Heaven at all. She'd merely stopped off there on her way to Hell. Miss Lockharte opened her eyes to find Miss Merrihew and her brother standing over her, shouting at each other. At least they were both dead, too, and couldn't make any other young woman's life miserable and short. She wondered just what she had done so wrong in her twenty years that she deserved to be tormented in eternity.

Rosellen blinked, hoping to have even the suffocating clouds back, but no, the two sets of beady eyes were still there, the prune faces, the nasal, whining voices. They both wore black, relieved only by the reverend's white neckcloth, which was tied almost tall enough to hide his weak chin. The vultures had come, Rosellen thought, come to peck at her. Well, she wouldn't listen. She might be in Hell, but no one could force her to hold conversation with the other fiends. She didn't think so, at any rate.

"I don't care what her condition," Miss Merrihew was insisting. "I want her out of here."

For once Rosellen agreed with the headmistress, but she didn't believe either of their wishes would hold any weight in purgatory.

Mr. Merrihew was arguing that tossing her out wasn't good enough. "The wench will talk. She knows too much. With the epidemic and the school shut, who is to know what happens to the bitch?"

"All those other people she wrote to, that's who. We don't even know the half of them, or what she said. I just want her away from my school."

"But she can ruin us."

"Not if she hasn't already, and not if she knows what's good for her."

Rosellen thought it might be good for her to convince these

two demons to leave her alone, that she had no interest in spending eternity listening to their ghoulish grievances. "Go to Heaven," she said with a weak giggle at her own wit.

Miss Merrihew looked down and jabbed her bony finger into Rosellen's chest. "Aha, so you *were* pretending to be asleep! I knew it, you sly, deceitful chit. You've played that hand one too many times, missy."

With each word she spoke the headmistress poked at Rosellen again, until she felt like a pincushion, a live pincushion. "I . . . I . . . didn't die?"

"Why, I'll bet you were never sick at all, just malingering to avoid your duties. You are an ungrateful wretch, Miss Lockharte," Miss Merrihew shouted. "I was the only one who would take you in after your disgraceful conduct in London. I should have known better, but your uncle begged me. *He* didn't want you and now I understand why. You are not to be trusted, and I will not keep a viper like you next to my bosom."

One more sharp jab and Rosellen would not have any bosom at all. She tried to roll out of range, but the spadelike finger kept digging into her flesh. All she could manage was a confused whimper.

"Well you might snivel, you conniving hussy, but that will avail you nothing. I won't keep you here for another day. You are dismissed, Miss Lockharte, terminated, turned off. You have been disloyal, dishonest, and a bad influence on the students."

"And her handwriting has deteriorated considerably, too," Mr. Merrihew put in. "Not at all up to the standards of the Select Academy."

"Quite right, Jonas. I am ashamed that anyone saw those dreadful scribbles." Miss Merrihew crossed her arms over her own flat chest, to Rosellen's relief, but the headmistress was not finished. "How dare you send those letters behind my back? And how dare you tell me how to run my school, as if some impertinent chit from a vicarage knows the first thing about educating proper young ladies. And writing to Lord

Vance! Why, I am mortified that one of my instructors should bother our patron with such nitpicky complaints."

Ah, Rosellen thought, her memory jogged by the grating voice, like chalk on the blackboard, like pencil and pen scratching out line after line on parchment, *those* letters.

"Don't you know your place at all, girl?" Miss Merrihew shouted. "You will soon, for it is not here. I want you gone by morning."

Morning? Rosellen hadn't thought to live till morning. Obviously she had. It remained to be seen whether she'd live through another day, which, from the smirk on Mr. Merrihew's thin lips, was not a foregone conclusion. The sooner she was away from the school, the better, if only she could hold her head up. "I . . . I don't think I can manage, ma'am."

"Humph! Miss Prunes and Prisms doesn't think she can manage, Jonas! This is not a hotel, miss. You've already been in the infirmary for two weeks without doing a bit of work, and that is two weeks too long. I've paid for the physician, the medicine, and the servants to wait on you. That, of course, will come out of your last quarter's salary. No, I do not care if you drag your sorry self through the streets, you'll be off the premises and out of my sight tomorrow morning. I'd toss you out tonight, but I know what's proper."

While Rosellen's mind was spinning, she could hear hasty whispers above her.

". . . out of town," the hatchet-faced cleric was urging. "We don't want her wandering around Worthing talking to anyone."

Miss Merrihew nodded. "Thank you for reminding me of my Christian duty, Jonas. Out of the goodness of my heart, Miss Lockharte, and not because I think you deserve it, I shall order the school's cart to deliver you to Brighton in the morning. There you may find employment or you may fall by the wayside. I do not care which."

Rosellen knew she could not possibly leave in the morning. Where would she go? She had to make plans for her future, now that she was to have one, and she had to regain some of her strength. Her fuddled mind might be clearing, but she was still weak as a thrice-brewed tea leaf. As far as she could gather, she'd been lying there for two weeks, in a fever, a drugged stupor, or a near comatose sleep of exhaustion. She'd had precious little in the way of food, water, or exercise. She doubted she could comb her hair, much less take a cart to Brighton.

"I . . . I should like to stay a day or two longer, Miss Merrihew, with your permission. I can pay for my keep."

"And I should like to know how, missy." Miss Merrihew smiled. A shark's grin held more congeniality.

"I have fifty pounds."

Mr. Merrihew snickered. "Where would the likes of you be getting fifty pounds?"

"From the messenger who came. He must have been sent from my uncle." Rosellen wasn't clear on all the details or on precisely how many letters she did write.

Miss Merrihew shook her head, not disturbing a single hair of her tightly braided bun. "No messenger came for you. Your uncle certainly never wrote. He washed his hands of you two years ago, lucky man."

"There was a messenger," Rosellen insisted, "in gold livery. He came in a grand carriage."

"You were delirious, girl. Imagining things, the same as you imagined all those other accusations you made." Miss Merrihew looked pointedly toward her brother, the corrupt cleric. "No one will believe you."

Rosellen was scrabbling around in her rumpled bedclothes, searching for the pouch she remembered. "Fanny brought it up. She can tell you."

"Fanny was dismissed this afternoon for insubordination. I cannot have my maids going behind my back, accepting bribes to disobey my rules. She was off the school grounds without permission. That would have been enough to cost her her position, without her flirting with tradesmen to do your dirty work. No, she is gone, and you will be gone. That is final." Miss

Merrihew took her brother's arm on the way out of the room. As she passed through the door, almost out of Rosellen's sight, she called back, "And do not expect to be waited on like visiting royalty anymore. If you want something, you can jolly well fetch it yourself."

Rosellen wanted her money back.

Chapter Nine

Rosellen was right; she couldn't manage. Miss Merrihew
was right; she'd be gone. The headmistress sent Cook to help.
Cook was a large, wild-haired woman in a soiled apron who
smelled of stale cabbage.

"Tell folks there be vermin in my kitchens, will you?" She
pulled the brush through Rosellen's hair as if she were pluck-
ing a chicken, then tied it back with a string from her pocket—
one that might have trussed that same chicken, Rosellen thought
with a shudder. Then her coarse hands stripped off Rosellen's
nightgown and tugged a crumpled gray uniform over her head.
Woolen stockings, a limp chip straw bonnet, and worn shoes
completed Rosellen's ensemble. "Say as how I serve tainted
meat and pocket the difference?"

"I only suggested to Miss Merrihew . . ."

Cook propped Rosellen against a wall, not quite acciden-
tally bumping her head. Rosellen sank down as if her knees
were made of mashed potatoes, without Cook's lumps. She
could only watch from the floor as the angry servant crammed
her belongings into a satchel, tossing Rosellen a flimsy spencer.

"I ain't no fancy Frenchified chef, but I set a decent table.
Not good enough for a fine lady like you, eh? Where's all your

fine airs now, missy, that's what I'd like to know. You'll be missing my cooking soon enough, I'll warrant, when you ain't got no breakfast in your stomach."

Rosellen struggled into the light wrap, for she was already chilled, no fire having been lit in the sickroom. She felt sick to her stomach, too, wondering what was to happen to her. No, she wasn't going to miss Cook's greasy eggs and burned toast.

Cook slammed Rosellen's lap desk into her arms, then pulled the drooping girl to her feet. She half pushed, half pulled Miss Lockharte down the stairs and out the back door, where Jake was waiting with the school's pony cart. Cook tossed Rosellen and her possessions into the back of the cart, on the bare wooden slats, next to some empty crates.

There was no good-bye, no hamper of food for the journey, not even Fanny's address. Jake, the academy's man-of-all-work, didn't know it either.

"It's a rum go for both of you, I be thinking, miss," he said, handing a blanket back to Rosellen when he saw how she was shivering in her thin clothes. It was the horse's blanket, she realized instantly, but welcome all the same. She huddled under it, queasy from the cart's jolting movement, wondering if she was better off now that she wasn't dead.

Jake helped her out of the cart when they reached the coaching inn at Brighton. She would have fallen except for his arm at her waist. He guided her to a bench outside the busy inn and placed her satchel and the desk next to her. "I don't know what's to become of you, miss, and that's a fact. But iffen I don't get back before nuncheon with the supplies, it'll mean my job, too."

"I understand, Jake. You've been more than kind."

He pressed a coin into her hand. "It ain't much, miss, but you was always decent, unlike them other teachers what thought they were better'n fresh bread. It ain't fair what they done to you, Miss Lockharte, but I can't make it right."

Rosellen looked down. The silver crown must be a fortune to Jake. She couldn't accept it. With a trembling arm, she held it out. "No, Jake, I'll be fine. I'll just sit here and catch my breath and decide what's to be done. You keep it."

Jake backed away, touching the brim of his cap. "No, miss, I couldn't sleep nights, was I to leave you like that."

He did manage to leave her without the horse blanket. He couldn't let old Posy go cold, now, could he? Rosellen sat on the bench, too numb to shiver. She'd stay a little longer, gathering her wits, her stamina, and her courage. She couldn't gather what she did not have, though. Lud, what was to become of her?

She looked at the silver in her hand. One crown. Five shillings. She could purchase a cup of tea and a roll. She could use it to send a plea to Uncle Townsend. Or she could offer it to the next wagon driver that came by, in exchange for a ride. But to where?

Miss Lockharte needed her fifty pounds. With that much blunt she could afford a clean room nearby while she regrouped. Then she could travel to London and find a decent position if her uncle would not take her back. With fifty pounds she could even buy passage to the Colonies, where there were more opportunities. That's what she would do, Rosellen thought; she'd go to America and make a fresh start. Surely someone in that vast land needed a governess or a schoolteacher or a fair hand. Of course there were savages there, but who could be more barbaric than the Merrihew siblings? She'd do it, Rosellen decided, as soon as she got back her fifty pounds.

First she had to find Fanny. Fanny could swear to the magistrate that there really had been a messenger and money. The maid could tell the authorities where the pouch had come from, and perhaps where it had gone. Rosellen didn't think the gift was from her uncle Townsend, for he was too parsimonious. He wouldn't have sent so much blunt, he wouldn't have sent a carriage, and he wouldn't have his footmen wearing expensive livery and powder-tax wigs. Rosellen needed Fanny to remember if there had been a crest on the door or a message. At least the maid could tell her who else had received letters, for the whole of the last fortnight was a foggy blur in Rosellen's mind. She did have a niggling suspicion in the haze of her memory that Fanny couldn't read, but she'd face that later. First she had to find the girl.

When one of the ostlers passed her bench, she asked where she might find the local constable. She would lay the charges with him, she decided, and let him locate Fanny for her. The stableboy gave her the directions and said she might leave her belongings on the bench, for Rosellen didn't think she had the strength to carry a tune, much less a cherrywood lap desk.

As she was making her slow, unsteady way across the innyard, Rosellen could hear some kind of commotion, but it had nothing to do with her, so she kept going, picking her path through the stableyard litter. Then, just as she was about to reach the high street and its clean sidewalks, she heard the racket and rumble of a fast-moving vehicle, the shouts and shrieks of frantic bystanders. She looked back to see a pair of enormous dray horses pulling a wagon of enormous ale kegs enormously close to her. What fool was driving so recklessly? she wondered, then saw that no one was. The horses were runaways, frightened by the screaming, scurrying crowds.

Rosellen had nowhere to go and couldn't get there on her wobbly legs. She tried to back up, closer to the building, but her foot slipped on a pile of manure. She fell to the ground, sure she had been saved from the influenza only to succumb to a stampede.

"Is she dead?" she heard someone ask. This time Rosellen decided she'd wait for someone to tell her.

"No, the horses missed her," another voice responded, "and the wagon wheels went to either side of the chit. Damnedest thing I ever seen. And what set them horses off like that is a plumb mystery, too."

"Then why ain't she moving?"

Rosellen could feel rough hands on her arms and legs, probing for damages. At her weak protest, she was instantly hauled to her feet, but she couldn't stand for the life of her and collapsed back to the dirt.

A worried voice asked, "What'll we do, boss, take her inside the inn?"

"The missus has gone off to visit her sister. There's no female to tend to her. She's one of the teachers from that girls' school, though. I seen Jake bring her. We'll take her back and let them tend to her there."

This time they carried her up to the attic room. Battered and bruised, Rosellen didn't have enough energy to groan. If she could have moved, she would have changed out of her befouled gown. Now she smelled the way she felt. At least there was some water by the bedside and a cup, although she didn't want to think of how long either had been there. She didn't want to think at all, so she sipped the water, then let her mind drift into the by-now familiar gray haze. Life had definitely been easier when she was dead.

"You fool, now she's back!" Miss Merrihew was shouting, seemingly from a distance. "We could have been rid of her once and for all."

Rosellen recognized Mr. Merrihew's querulous accent. "Don't blame that on me. My hands are clean."

They wouldn't be for long if he stayed in this room, Rosellen thought. The attic chamber was so small, a speck of dirt covered half the floor. Heaven knew what she'd trailed in from the stableyard. Rosellen decided to feign a coma—which wasn't going to take any great acting—rather than engage in another pointless confrontation with this evil pair. Besides, she might learn something to her benefit. Heaven knew she needed every advantage she could glean.

Mr. Merrihew was going on. "I didn't do anything to the chit this morning. And I wasn't the one who took her in again this afternoon."

"What did you expect me to do with the men from the livery stable showing up at the same time that Lord and Lady Manley were delivering their brat back at school? The jackanapes were standing there with the twit propped up between them, grinning like they'd found my missing pot of gold. Waiting for a reward, more likely. Hah! Hell will freeze over first."

"Couldn't you have said she was on her way somewhere?"

"Look at her, you gudgeon. The only place she is headed to is the midden heap. Besides, turning the gel away in front of the Manleys would have hurt the academy's reputation as badly as anything the fool could say. We are supposed to be teaching the Golden Rule, recall? You ought to, for it's the only class you teach, Jonas. Can't you remember to sound like a vicar occasionally? You didn't have to mumble that bit about a bad penny right where Lord Manley could hear. Besides, did you listen to those men say she was asking about the constable? That's all we need, with the students returning, an officer of the law asking awkward questions."

"So what will you do now?"

"What will *we* do, don't you mean? I'll have to think about it. For now I intend to leave her right here, so the Manley chit can't write to Papa with any foolish notions. The girls liked the wench; they might take it amiss if we toss the baggage out with the trash. But who knows what might happen to poor Miss Lockharte in her weakened condition?"

"If we're lucky."

"Luck has nothing to do with it." Miss Merrihew pried Rosellen's clenched fingers open and extracted the silver crown piece. "This ought to cover my expenses until we can figure out some other way of getting rid of the nuisance without stirring up a bumblebroth."

Rosellen listened to their footsteps recede on the bare floor, then the narrow stairs. She opened her eyes and scowled after the unholy pair. Now she was a nuisance? Like a fly one took a swatter to? She doubted if they'd be back this day, so she could rest for a bit, but only a bit. One thing was certain: She'd die for real if she stayed there in the attic with no food and no fire. Rosellen did *not* want to expire smelling of the stables. That truly would have added insult to injury. She'd had enough of both.

When she woke up again, her mind was not so fuddled; thus, she felt it was time to make a plan. Considering she had absolutely no resources, her options were remarkably simple. She could stay there and starve or she could leave—and starve. Rosellen was hungry, which she took to be a good sign. So she decided to leave via the kitchens and fetch herself some bread and cheese. Lud knew she'd paid for them, with her fifty pounds and five shillings. Also, someone in the kitchens might know Fanny's whereabouts. She'd have to avoid Cook and the Merrihews, of course, and find some form of conveyance back to Brighton. Since the local officer of the law was Lord Vance, he of the midnight trysts with Miss Merrihew, Rosellen knew she had to go farther afield to present her case.

Miss Lockharte congratulated herself on the excellence of her scheme. Now all she had to do was execute it, which she admitted was a poor choice of words, considering the circumstances. Besides, considering that she couldn't raise her head off the pillow, this was easier said than done. She rolled over until her feet were off the bed. That was a start. With agonizing slowness, Rosellen made the rest of her aching body follow. She could almost hear her joints creak their protest, saying they were not about to hold her up, not without a lot of encouragement. So, while she was on her knees on the dirty floor, she said a prayer.

"Dear Lord"—she began the way her father had taught her, expressing gratitude for her blessings—"thank you for saving me from the epidemic and the wild horses. I wouldn't want your efforts on my behalf to go for naught, so if you could just see your way clear to lending a bit more assistance, I would greatly appreciate it. If you'll help me down the stairs, I can take it from there, I think."

Clinging to the bedpost, Rosellen levered herself to a standing position. This time her knees did cooperate enough to keep her upright, if she hung on to something. Luckily, the room was so small that she could reach from the bed to the wall to the door frame to the bannister. One step down, two. Her head was spinning again, but she could do it. She had to do it. Three steps . . . four. How many of the blasted things were there?

Too many. She had to rest at the landing, gasping for air, clutching the railing as if it were a lifeline. But she'd made it out of the attic story. Now the steps were wider and deeper, with carpeting. She wouldn't have to hold on so tightly, thank goodness, for her cold fingers were growing numb.

Rosellen started counting again at the next set of stairs, this time out loud. So she never heard the footsteps behind her or the *whoosh* of air as hands reached out and gave her back a forceful shove. There were three more flights of stairs, with fourteen steps each, and Rosellen hit each and every one of them before landing in a heap at the bottom.

So God did answer prayers, Rosellen thought, even if His response wasn't quite what she'd had in mind. Now she prayed that the ominous crack she'd heard was the bannister, not her wrist. While she was at it, before losing consciousness, Rosellen prayed for help, for she wasn't getting any farther without divine intervention—or someone's.

Chapter Ten

*H*elp was on the way, a circuitous, slow way to be sure, but it was on the way.

The Heatherstone brothers went on a detour at Woking, where they heard about an illegal prizefight being held behind an inn's stable. Timothy backed the winner; Thomas backed one of the tavern wenches into an empty stall. A fair was on in Guildford, so they had to stay to see the two-headed calf, the sword swallower, and the rope climber. Opportunities like that didn't come every day. With a pocketful of coins, Thomas won a handful of pinchbeck jewelry at the games. With a slightly larger purse, Timothy won the temporary affections of the tattooed lady. An opportunity like that didn't come every day either.

There was to be a cockfight at Horsham that night, so the brothers stayed on. Miss Lockharte must be dead by now, so another day or two couldn't make any difference to her. Neither of the twins was feeling hexed or haunted by her wandering wraith, so what was the rush to hear bad news? The longer they waited to sign up, the better the chance of old Boney being defeated without their assistance, which suited them to a cow's thumb. The following morning, waking in a cow's manger, heads pounding and pockets considerably lighter, the twins decided that such delays did not suit Miss Lockharte's spirit. If the female was indeed starting to take her revenge, they'd better hurry.

So they raced as if the devil were on their heels, or a dishonored woman. At Horsham, the careening curricles took a narrow bridge. The wheels locked and Tim went flying. Tom brought his horses under control, then went back to untangle his brother's cattle. Lastly, he fished his twin out of the water. He couldn't save Tim's hat, which was floating downstream at a merry pace. One of Tom's horses was lamed, and Tim's curricle was damaged. They'd have to head slowly for Cuckfield, where someone could make repairs and where Tim could buy a new hat.

Lord Haverhill saw no reason to hurry. If his niece was dead, she was dead. No one else was going to pay to put her in the ground, so she'd keep until he got to that wretched school. And if she wasn't dead, there was nothing he could do to nurse a sick female. Besides, the baron meant to enjoy this vacation from his high-strung daughter and low-spirited spouse. His coach was well sprung, well protected by outriders, and well stocked from the Haverhill pantry. The coachman knew to avoid bumps and high speeds, for the baron hated to be jostled around like a cricket in a cage. The driver also knew to be on the lookout for inns that catered to the quality, for the baron did love his food and drink.

They stopped outside Reigate at noontime, at the Quiet Woman. What could be more fortuitous? The meal was superb, the wines obviously smuggled. Afterward, Baron Haverhill needed a nap. He might as well stay on at the delightful place for dinner, which the innkeep promised would surpass luncheon. The serving wench was surpassing lovely, too. With tasty morsels all around, Rosellen's uncle decided to stay the night rather than face the irksome duty of arranging a funeral.

* * *

Viscount Stanford was riding. He didn't like being confined for hours, no matter how comfortable his carriage. He didn't enjoy riding through sleet and rain either, so the luxurious crested coach was following at a more leisurely pace in case the weather turned inclement.

He, too, intended to enjoy this freedom from the obligations that were burdening him in Town. Fine horseflesh beneath him, clear skies above, Wynn's family and the War Office were miles away. Unfortunately, a man could not outride his thoughts.

Was he truly an uncaring beast? Did he really show callous disdain for those beneath him? Wynn took stock. His servants were the highest paid in London, with the least work, there were so many of them. His tenant farmers lived better than many lords. His cottagers had schools and doctors and new roofs whenever they needed. Even his mines were the safest in England, with no children employed. He did have his sister's best interests to heart, no matter what she thought, and he took the rest of his responsibilities equally seriously, from serving in Parliament to sending donations to orphanages.

But Miss Lockharte was dying and he could not recall meeting her. Perhaps he had shown carelessness in not clarifying his refusal to employ her, but Wynn was not in the habit of explaining his actions to anyone. He hadn't been wrong in the matter, he decided, just in the method. Mushrooms and hangers-on did not deserve his consideration; unfortunate, downtrodden schoolteachers did. According to his sister, at any rate.

Wynn could not correlate his sister's meek, mousy creature with the author of the damning diatribe he'd received. According to the letter, he was a condescending, conceited, cockleheaded coxcomb who had hurt another human being without noticing, which was worse than doing it on purpose and not something to be proud of. Wynn Alton did not want to be that person.

* * *

Rosellen knew she wasn't dead. She hurt too much. She also knew she'd never leave this attic room alive. Luckily, she didn't think the Merrihews meant to kill her immediately, not with Miss Manley playing Lady Bountiful once a day with an apple or a biscuit. In fact, if she hadn't fallen practically at Miss Manley's feet, Rosellen suspected, the Merrihews would simply have swept her crumpled body out the door like a dust ball. But with the curious students returning to school, how many "accidents" could one instructor be expected to suffer?

And Rosellen was suffering mightily. Her head was concussed, she supposed, making her see double, with both views spinning nauseatingly. Her arm was splinted and swollen, and every other inch of her was black and blue. She would have taken laudanum gladly, but none was provided. She would have traded her mother's lap desk to be clean again, but no one would fetch the tub and the cans of water. Perhaps she was fortunate in that, Rosellen considered, for the Merrihews might decide to drown her in a hip bath. Unfortunately, she still stank of horse. At least she was in her own nightgown, out of her soiled, torn uniform. A maid had helped her, a new girl who refused to talk to her on the headmistress's orders. She brought a pitcher of water, a bowl of porridge, and a hardened slice of toast. Cook's culinary efforts had not improved; neither had her temper.

Rosellen's prospects had dwindled from poor to nonexistent. With her right wrist broken, she could neither teach penmanship nor hire herself out as a secretary. She couldn't even write to Uncle Townsend, begging for his nonexistent mercy. What in Heaven's name was to become of her? And did Heaven care anymore?

Rosellen was beyond tears and almost beyond hope.

The rain started just beyond Worthing. Wynn switched to the carriage, tying his chestnut stallion in the back. He should have left Jupiter behind with the groom, who was supposed to be on the lookout for the Heatherstone twins, Baron Haverhill, and Tripp Hayes, none of whom were where they were supposed to be.

Red-haired identical twins would make a stir even in Brighton, where His Royal Flamboyance was a byword. No one had seen the Heatherstone heirs, not at the hotels, not at the gaming parlors, not at the clubs. Wynn had checked the coffeehouses while his driver and groom canvassed the livery stables. There were no rumors of cockfights, mills, or races, nothing to take those hellborn blockheads out of town.

Tripp Hayes was not at his family's estate in Bognor Regis. His mother hadn't seen him, didn't expect him, and couldn't imagine why his friend the viscount thought dear Thorence would leave London during the Season. Wynn couldn't imagine one good reason for his old school chum's valet to lie to him. No honest reason, anyway.

And Baron Haverhill had not driven through Worthing on his way to that girls' school. The place was too small for the locals not to keep count of every carriage and cart that passed through. Wynn's own arrival had been noted by no less than fourteen persons raking their yards, hanging their wash, sweeping their front stoops.

Deuce take it, there was nothing left to do except visit Susan's friend or her grave. He'd come this far and he had a blasted bouquet of flowers in a bucket.

Wynn could not recall what made Miss Merrihew's Select Academy for Young Females of Distinction the school of choice for the promising buds of the *belle monde*. Miss Merrihew herself was everything the viscount disliked in a person. She was stiff and angular, sharp-faced yet sugar-tongued. She was an insincere, toadying sycophant who thought his presence added to her consequence, while she bullied the servant who answered the door. She eyed the flowers in his hand with an avaricious gleam, then led him into a sumptuous private parlor and tried to ply him with tea and cakes. He refused.

"I am sorry to disappoint you, my lord," she was saying

now, her artificial smile giving the lie to the least hint of regret. "It is too, too gracious of you to inquire, but Miss Lockharte is no longer with us."

"I am sorry for your loss." Wynn mouthed the proper, polite phrases. Meanwhile, he was hiding an unexpected pang of sorrow for the bright, impassioned flame that had been snuffed out. Miss Lockharte may have been misguided, but she had been no fawning flatterer. And now he would never get to make amends.

"It's no great loss, I can assure you," Miss Merrihew replied with a sniff. "Miss Lockharte was an insolent, outspoken young person who did not know her place."

That Wynn could well believe. "When did she pass on then?" he asked for his sister's sake.

"Pass on?" the headmistress repeated. "The twit didn't die." Wynn could have sworn he heard her mutter, "More's the pity," before she concluded, "I meant she is no longer on the staff here at the Select Academy. She was dismissed for insubordination."

Why should he feel so relieved? He smiled at himself for growing tenderhearted over a totty-headed female. He nodded toward the flowers still in his hand. "I was led to believe she was ailing. My sister was concerned enough to ask me to stop by while I was in Brighton on business."

Miss Merrihew waved a bony hand. "La, a trifling indisposition." She was not about to discuss a virulent epidemic at her school, in case this gentleman of the first stare knew the parents of prospective students. She was also not about to give credence to anything else he might have heard concerning Miss Lockharte. "I fear the fever did seem to affect her senses, however. Quite addled her brain, in fact, so she became delusional with wild talk of robbers and assassins."

"And you sent her away?"

The woman shrugged pointy shoulders. "What else could I do? I had the welfare of my dear students to consider."

And their papas' purses, Wynn added to himself. Dash it,

now he'd have to track the female down to make sure she was established properly. He stood. "Then if you'd be kind enough to give me her address, I won't be taking any more of your time."

"Nonsense, my lord, you must stay to tea. I absolutely insist on it. The wretched girl should be here any minute with the tray. It's raining dreadfully, besides. You cannot wish to leave yet." Or before Jonas returned. Who knew what an influential nobleman like the viscount could do for her brother's career?

Wynn did not resume his seat. "Too kind. But I'll just get the address and be on my way."

Miss Merrihew gnashed her teeth. That troublemaking twit was not going to spew her lies into this handsome Corinthian's ears. "I am afraid I couldn't give you her direction, my lord."

Couldn't or wouldn't? Wynn wondered. Something did not ring true. He studied one of the roses in his hand. The petals were beginning to brown at the edges. If he didn't get to Miss Lockharte soon, the flowers would be totally wilted. "Miss Merrihew, do you realize that one word from me would see at least twenty of your students withdrawn? Those are the ones I can think of first, of course; there might be more. The Harrington-Wyte chit, the under-secretary's two daughters, the Manley girl . . ."

"She's upstairs." The false smile was replaced by a clenched jaw.

Wynn raised an eyebrow.

"There was an accident in Brighton when she was departing. She was brought back here." Miss Merrihew went to the door, patently ready enough now to see the last of him.

He did not move. "I would see her."

"I am not running a blasted hotel!" Then she recalled the Harrington-Wyte chit, the under-secretary's two daughters . . . "That is, I'm sorry, my lord, it is not possible for you to see Miss Lockharte. Her wits became even more addled after the unfortunate incident in the coachyard. She took to ranting and raving and dashing about. She had a slight spill on the stairs, so now we have to keep her confined in her room so she does not injure herself further. We are, ah, awaiting word from her relations about placing her in Bethlehem hospital." Miss Merrihew smiled again, genuinely this time. What a good idea! She'd have her brother make the arrangements this very afternoon, as soon as she got rid of this nosy nonpareil.

Bedlam? Wynn shook his head. In her letter, the female had seemed determined to be heard, not demented. Besides, a mental institution was no place for a gentlewoman, no matter how low she had fallen. "You'd consign a sick female to an asylum?" he asked, wondering what he could do about it.

"What would you have me do, my lord? I am running a school, not a hospital. I think I have been more than generous in letting her stay on so long when she is not even in my employ."

"I am sure you have been everything that's charitable and considerate, madam," he said, sure of anything but. "I'd like to see her for myself."

"Impossible," the woman snapped, entirely out of patience. "No gentlemen are permitted upstairs."

"Surely you cannot think there is anything improper about my visiting Miss Lockharte for a moment, to wish her well and give her my sister's regards and flowers. I will be sure to leave the door open," he added dryly.

Miss Merrihew crossed her arms over her flat chest, a stance that usually sent students and instructors alike scurrying. "No."

Wynn plucked a rose petal. "Miss Manley." Another. "Cousin Lucy's eldest. No, the middle daughter."

Miss Merrihew bit her thin lip. Before another petal hit the floor, she hissed, "This way."

She led him through a slightly less sumptuous parlor, then up a flight of stairs. He could hear girlish giggles and see heads disappearing behind doors at their approach, but they went up more stairs. An older female in a gray uniform and spectacles saw them approach the next landing. She screeched and fled back into her room. Still they climbed. The staircase was winding around, narrower and darker, without carpeting. The railing was rough enough to leave splinters, so Wynn did not use it. Miss Merrihew was panting. They went higher. When they could go no more, Wynn had to duck his head to get under the rafters. His unwilling guide plowed a path through empty trunks, discarded desks, and piles of books to a door with an even lower lintel. Miss Merrihew threw the door open without knocking, then stepped back. "Here, my lord, you wanted to see for yourself. Look."

Wynn bent over and entered the room. No, it was more a closet. Perhaps someone had kept pigeons there once. It smelled like it. He took a handkerchief out of his pocket to hold over his nose while he continued his survey. There was a narrow bed and a washstand that leaned against the wall and hooks hammered into the rafters to hold clothes, he supposed, though none were hanging. On the floor were a satchel, a crumpled gray rag like the one that other teacher had been wearing, and a lady's lap desk. On the night table were a chipped pitcher, a piece of bread with green showing on the edges, and an apple core. But on the bed, ah, on the bed was an even more dismal sight. Wynn took out his quizzing glass to get a better look, then was sorry he did.

He had never seen a sadder scrap of humanity than the female under a threadbare cover, not in the orphanages he supported or the poorhouses he financed, not even in London's stews when he'd had to travel through them. "Lud," he said, "I thought you told me she wasn't dead."

Chapter Eleven

Rosellen reluctantly opened her eyes, knowing that the room would start spinning again. What she saw was not encouraging. "I *am* dead," she groaned. "And here is Beelzebub. Twofold."

Miss Merrihew gasped, whether from Rosellen's impertinence or the climb up the stairs, it wasn't clear, but the viscount only murmured, "Ah, just as sweet-spoken as I imagined from your letter."

"I am sorry, but I am quite out of honeyed phrases, Lord Stanford. And do pardon me for not curtsying."

"At least your mind is in one piece, if you remember me."

Remember him? How did one forget the man who'd ruined one's life, especially when he was the most attractive man in all of England? And the rudest. Now, at the worst moment in her existence, he had to reappear. Rosellen groaned again. Here she was, in her dingy nightgown, with her hair like a squirrel's nest and her face like a baboon's behind—and those were the high points of her appearance. She was at low tide. No, she was the flotsam and jetsam that got left at low tide, shipwrecked, capsized, sunk. There he was, thinking he could walk on water again.

Stanford was as handsome as she recalled. His dark hair was wavy, his nose was straight, his jaw was square with a cleft in it. He was dressed with casual elegance, in buckskin breeches that stretched across well-muscled thighs and a bottle-green coat that must have been molded to his broad shoulders. The only faults Rosellen could see, doubled at that, were the stooped posture he seemed to have acquired and the quizzing glass that made his brown eye enlarged and grotesque. Of all the arrogant affectations, that was the worst. She didn't mind the scented handkerchief, only wishing she had one, or the diamond in his neckcloth, which could have kept her for a year. She minded the quizzing glass. She was viewing his magnificence twice, while the dastard was magnifying her imperfections tenfold.

"I hate you," she managed to get out past the lump in her throat. She swallowed hard. The imperious ass might see her in dire straits; she'd be damned before she let him see her in tears.

"Now you understand why I didn't want you to visit the creature, my lord," Miss Merrihew crowed. "Her wits have obviously gone begging, just as I said. The girl is demented."

Or honest. Wynn couldn't remember the last time anyone had disliked him so. He ducked lower against the sloping eaves and took a step closer to the bed. "Miss Lockharte, I am sorry you feel that way, and I am sorry for your plight. Do you need anything?"

Rosellen could have laughed, if her lip weren't swollen. She was destitute, disabled, and in danger of her life. What could she possibly need from this popinjay who had everything? "Get out."

He nodded. "I do not wish to add to your distress, ma'am. I just wanted to bring my sister's best regards and these flowers."

Wynn held out the bouquet, then realized that one of Miss Lockharte's hands was bound to a board and the other, sticking out of a frayed cuff, looked as frail as a reed. He looked around for someplace to put the blasted nosegay. This was the last time he'd listen to his sister, he told himself, and definitely the last time he'd have anything to do with crackbrained spinsters. He settled for putting the flowers on the bed next to her. At least she could smell them there, which had to improve her condition somewhat. He'd leave some money with the beldam behind him in the doorway. Susan would have to be content with that. "I'll be going then."

Miss Merrihew's relief was obvious as she asked him again to stay for tea. Wynn turned to follow her out, his mission concluded as unsatisfactorily as everything else recently, but then he looked back and saw the tear. A solitary drop of moisture was rolling down the penmanship instructor's empurpled cheek, traveling from a closed black eye to a cut and scraped chin. Wynn gently touched the hand that lay limply on the cover. "Miss Lockharte?"

Rosellen was not totally attics to let. Viscount Stanford was obviously the heaven-sent answer to her prayers. Heaven must have a quirky sense of humor, indeed, for he was not the answer she wanted. The elegant Stanford was there, though, in the ramshackle room of a ragtag schoolmarm. That was miracle enough. She could not afford to send him away, not even if her pride was the only thing she had left to lose. Rosellen licked her swollen lip, tasting the salty tear, and whispered, "Please, sir, I need help."

Wynn turned toward Miss Merrihew. "Do you know, I believe I will take tea after all, here with Miss Lockharte."

"Here?" she squawked. "You cannot stay here!"

"Certainly I can. It's not what I am accustomed to, but if Miss Lockharte can manage, I daresay I can muddle through."

"It . . . it isn't proper."

Wynn took out his quizzing glass again and gave the formidable dame a glance that reminded her of who he was. "If, as you said, Miss Lockharte is no longer in your employ, her reputation cannot be any concern of yours. We shall, of course, leave the door open." He thrust the bouquet of flowers into her hands. "And perhaps you would be so good as to find a vase for these when you order the tea."

As he took two steps closer to the bed, Wynn hit his head on a roof beam. "Blast!" he muttered, then, "Pardon."

Rosellen smiled on the inside, oddly relieved that he wasn't hunchbacked after all.

Rubbing his head, Wynn looked around. He couldn't stand, not without getting a permanent crick in his neck, and there was no chair. He shrugged, then sat on the none-too-clean floor next to the low bed. Thank goodness his valet was back in London. "Now, miss," he said, "how may I be of service?"

He was really going to help her! Rosellen was so overcome, she could hardly speak. She swallowed twice before managing to tell him, "I need to get to Brighton. Could you . . . would you take me?"

Perhaps she had family in Brighton, friends who would look after her better than she was being tended here. There were no jars of ointments for her cuts, no ice for the swelling, no lemonade or calf's-foot jelly, nothing one associated with the sickroom. Wynn saw an easy, speedy solution to the problem confronting him. "My pleasure, ma'am. I am headed that way myself. But are you sure you are up to making the trip? Those stairs alone"—he gestured toward the attic door—"seem too tortuous for one in your condition."

"Oh, I got down them all right last time. It was getting up that was the problem. It doesn't matter. I cannot stay here."

Wynn nodded. He didn't know how much longer he could tolerate the fetid room himself. "I agree that this is not the most healthful environment."

Rosellen made a sound almost like a chuckle. "That is why I have to get to the magistrate's office in Brighton. They're trying to kill me."

Wynn's heart sank. So much for a tidy resolution to the mess of Miss Lockharte. And so much for his hopes that Miss Merrihew had exaggerated the female's mental condition. She didn't have any friends in Brighton; she had a flea-brained notion to call in the constables. "Surely not," he said, trying to speak lightly. He was hoping to humor her out of a scheme that would see her in Bedlam before she could say "Jack Rabbit."

But she was going on. "Yes, they are. They pushed me down the stairs when they couldn't strangle or suffocate me. And they made those wild horses bolt, although I am not quite certain how."

"They . . . ?"

Rosellen understood his question. "The Merrihews, of course. Oh, and they stole my money."

"Miss Merrihew robbed you?" It seemed like a good place to start, Wynn thought. If he could make her see the absurdity of her accusations, perhaps there was hope for her after all.

"And her brother. That's why I need to get to Brighton, so the constable will find Fanny, who can explain." Rosellen knew she was speaking disjointedly, but she could see the disbelief on his face, on both faces. She closed her eyes to make the double image go away. She just had to make him understand, and she had to do it before Miss Merrihew returned or before she ran out of energy altogether. "Fanny was the maid here before they sent her away so she couldn't tell anyone about the money. If I find her, someone will have to listen to me."

"Miss Lockharte, have you considered that, if your coins have gone missing and the maid Fanny has gone missing, perhaps they are together?"

"No, not Fanny. She is a good girl and my friend. Besides, it wasn't a handful of coins; it was fifty pounds. And one crown, to be exact."

More delusions. Wynn sighed. "Miss Lockharte—"

The fingers of her unbound hand clenched the covers at her side. "I know what you are thinking: Where did this freakish female get fifty pounds? That's the problem. I'm not quite sure, but Fanny knows. I was feverish when the messenger came. By carriage. In a wig." She opened her eyes to see his reaction, then closed them quickly, before another tear could escape. "You don't believe me."

"I believe you were ill, desperately so. And you certainly took a fall. But to think that Miss Merrihew and her brother—he is that clerical fellow, isn't he?—tried to murder you for fifty pounds does not make sense."

"It wasn't about the money at first. They tried to kill me before it even arrived."

"Before . . . ?" he prompted.

She turned her face toward the wall. "It was because I wrote some letters."

Wynn cleared his throat. "I am well aware that you wrote letters, Miss— Good grief, never say you wrote one of *those* letters to your employers?"

She nodded, then groaned at the movement. "Both of them."

Wynn stood so quickly, he bumped his head again. Incredulous, he demanded, "What kind of blithering idiot would do such a thing?" Now he wanted to strangle her, too. "What did you expect to happen?"

"I expected to die, that's what!"

"And you believe in burning your bridges with a vengeance, don't you? Still, an apology ought to take care of the coil. The Merrihews cannot be without forgiveness. He's a religious chap, after all."

"No, you don't understand. I saw things here, knew information that could damage their reputations, ruin the school."

"And you threatened them with it?" he practically shouted.

"I thought I was dying," she repeated.

Wynn didn't know what to believe, what to think of this female. She was either the world's biggest fool or a raving maniac. He was relieved when a maid came to the door and coughed. She was holding a tray, looking for a place to set it. "I'll take that," Wynn said, nodding for her to leave. She scurried away like a frightened mouse. Most likely she thought Miss Lockharte was dicked in the nob, too, Wynn thought. He

95

set the tray down on the floor, noting that this could not be the offering he would have been served in the headmistress's private parlor. The teapot was earthenware, and the plate contained bread and butter and two slices of poppy-seed cake. Miss Lockharte was leaning over the bed, looking at the meager fare as if it were manna.

"Shall I pour?" he asked, already at the task. "Sugar?"

"Please." Rosellen licked her swollen lip.

"One or two lumps?"

"Four."

He placed a slice of cake in her good hand and watched while she struggled to bring it to her mouth. Deuce take it, she'd never manage the teacup. Feeling like the veriest nodcock, he bent almost double to set it next to her lips. She gulped audibly, then looked up. "I'm so glad you're here. They wouldn't poison *your* tea."

Lud, Wynn thought as he fed her the entire contents of the platter and half the pot of tea, she was starving. And she was stark raving mad.

Chapter Twelve

"*Y*ou cannot stay here." By the time Miss Lockharte had finished the last crumb, Lord Stanford had reached a decision.

Rosellen sighed with relief and repletion. "You do believe me then."

Wynn didn't believe a word of the preposterous prattle. The Merrihews were pillars of propriety. The sister was a well-respected educator of young females and the brother was a man of the cloth. They were not killers and cutpurses. This was a girls' school, by George, not a sinkhole of depravity. On the other hand, Miss Lockharte was certainly not in their good graces, to judge from Miss Merrihew's scowls, to say nothing of the treatment she was receiving in this airless cubbyhole, such as it was. To be fair, when the viscount dismissed an insolent servant, he did not expect to have to care for the chap forever either.

Well, the Merrihews wouldn't have to look after Miss Lockharte any longer. They hadn't done much of a job of it, Wynn thought angrily, and they were ready to send her off to an insane asylum. That *would* be murder. He was ready to send her to one of his lesser estates to recover. Lud knew he had enough pensioners; one more would not make a difference if she never got her health back or her wits.

Wynn told himself he'd do the same for any unfortunate soul, not just to appease a guilty conscience, and certainly not because, under the black and blue, the chit had turquoise eyes.

"I'll have my coachman return to fetch you as soon as the physician says you are well enough to travel."

"What physician? My lord, they did not call the doctor in, for they did not want me talking to him."

"Who wrapped your arm then?"

"Jake, the man-of-all-work."

She spoke so matter-of-factly, Wynn couldn't tell if the woman was telling the truth or another of her fanciful taradiddles. "And they didn't mind that you spoke to this Jake?" Lud, he was sounding like her now.

"Jake dares not speak out or he'll lose his own position, and he has three children to feed. It doesn't matter. I have to leave today."

"To see the constable in Brighton?"

"To see another sunrise."

She had a point, Wynn conceded. He could drive her to Brighton, where a doctor could look at her, to make sure Jake knew what he was about, and start her recovery there. He wouldn't have to cool his heels waiting either. She needed a nurse, that's what. He tried hard not to think of it as hiring a keeper, but he would leave Miss Lockharte in good hands and get on with his own investigations. He could send the carriage back for her in a week or two, to drive her to whichever estate seemed farthest away from people who might misinterpret her irrational ramblings.

"Very well." Wynn stood cautiously, wary of the beams. "I'll wait outside with the carriage. I do not relish another moment in Miss Merrihew's company any more than you do."

Rosellen was revitalized by the food and buoyed by her imminent rescue. She was not brave enough, however, to attempt those steps again. "My lord, would you mind waiting here in the attic? I, ah, don't think I am quite up to the stairs on my own."

"Of course you're not. I assumed Miss Merrihew would send that maid or someone up to assist you."

"No! She mustn't know I am leaving." Rosellen tried to grab for his hand but reached his coat hem instead. She hung on, as if to a lifeline. "She'll try to stop me, I know it!"

"Now that is definitely a delusion, miss. I believe she'll be happy to see the last of you."

Rosellen ignored his words. "But you'll wait here for me? You won't go down without me?"

Wynn patted her thin hand awkwardly, thankful again that his valet was in London, not seeing what damage was being done to one of Weston's finest creations. "I won't leave without you, Miss Lockharte. But can you manage to get ready on your own?"

Rosellen thought she could, if she kept her eyes closed and didn't make any sudden movements. She nodded, then moaned. She'd better not do that either. "If you'll just hand me my uniform and my satchel."

The rag on the floor was her dress? "This gray thing?"

"Yes, they took all of my other clothes away so—"

"Don't tell me, so you wouldn't run away." He placed the tattered gray fabric next to her, then found a shabby carpetbag under the bed. "Here you go. I'll be on the other side of the door."

Sweat beading on her forehead, Rosellen managed to get her stockings halfway up her calves. She decided to keep her nightgown on under her dress in lieu of a shift and because she was never going to get its narrow sleeve past her splinted wrist. She did get the despised uniform over her head before she fell off the bed.

Wynn heard the thud and the cry of pain. He dashed into the room and promptly smacked his head on the low beam. "Damn and blast!" Miss Lockharte was on the floor, struggling with her gown. Next thing he knew, she'd be claiming the thing attacked her. He got her to her feet, propped her up by the bedpost, and tugged the gown down. Despite the colorful bruises, her complexion was as gray as the gown. She looked even more miserable, if that were possible.

"Well, let's be off then." He tried to sound encouraging as he picked up the satchel.

"And my mother's lap desk?"

And the lap desk.

"Good." She nodded and immediately started to sink to the floor.

Wynn dropped the satchel—and the lap desk—and rushed to catch her. He cracked his head against the beam first. Dash it, he'd look as battered as the bacon-brained female in another half hour. They had to get out of there now. Without bothering to ask permission, he put one hand beneath Miss Lockharte's knees, the other around her back, and lifted. The woman weighed less than his saddle, by all that was holy. "I'll come back for your bag," he told her, starting the descent.

"And the lap desk?"

"And the lap desk. Heaven forfend you don't get to write any more letters." He could have sworn the burdensome female in his arms giggled.

When they reached the first landing, that same gray-haired, gray-gowned teacher was there.

"I never!" she declared, dropping her spectacles.

"I'm not surprised," Wynn said. Yes, that was definitely a giggle. If nothing else, Miss Lockharte had bottom, to be seeing the humor in a situation like this.

Then a parcel of schoolgirls popped their heads out of a classroom, their eyes huge in their heads, until a stern voice called, "Ladies!"

Miss Merrihew was waiting at the bottom. "You cannot do this, my lord."

"Why ever not?" Wynn was still holding Miss Lockharte in his arms; her weight was hardly noticeable even after the stairs. His major concern had been not to miss his footing and drop her. He didn't think her sticklike bones could stand another jarring.

"Why?" the headmistress spluttered. "Why? Because you cannot simply walk in here and carry away one of my instructors, that's why."

"But I thought you said she had been dismissed. In fact, I'm certain of it. You do not wish to stay on here, do you, Miss Lockharte, if Miss Merrihew reconsiders?"

Rosellen grabbed his collar even more firmly with her one good hand. That seemed to be answer enough for Wynn. "I thought not. We'll be going then."

Miss Merrihew was standing in the doorway now, arms crossed militantly over her chest. "No, I will not permit this . . . this outrageous behavior."

"More outrageous than not calling in a physician or providing proper nourishment? I think not, madam."

"Fabrications," she shrilled. "All fabrications. I told you she was nothing but a liar. The gel has been ill, that's all."

"And I am taking her to where she may convalesce, that's all."

Miss Merrihew's beady eyes narrowed. "And where might that be, my lord? I'm sure my brother, Reverend Merrihew, will not approve."

If his arms weren't full, Wynn would have taken out his quizzing glass, to depress any pretensions the stiff-rumped female might have that he gave a rap about her brother's approval or not. Instead he informed her, "I am first taking the lady to an inn between Worthing and Brighton. If your reverend brother wishes to discuss the matter with me, I have a few choice words I'd like to mention to him, such as faith, hope, and charity. Good day."

Miss Lockharte's whispered "Bravo" in his ear made Wynn

smile, until he realized they couldn't make the grand, triumphal exit she deserved; the front door was closed, for one thing, and they did not have their coats, for another. His was lying on a chair by the entry, with his hat and gloves on the paisley-covered table nearby.

"Where is your wrap?"

Rosellen had no idea what had become of her spencer after its encounter with the stableyard in Brighton. "I don't need one. Let us just go, please."

"Nonsense, it's rainy and damp outside, and you're already in poor health." He carefully lowered her onto the chair, pushing his own apparel aside.

Nothing was more important than getting out of this place. "If you must know, I gave my cloak to Fanny for mailing my letters."

Wynn just shook his head. "You gave her your only coat?"

"I told you, I thought I was dying. I didn't think I'd need a mantle where I was going, and Fanny did."

"You didn't think at all, it seems. I've never seen such a one as you for rash behavior."

"Such a fool, you mean."

He didn't answer, too busy trying to decide which of his estates was farthest away from his impressionable sister. Susan was excitable enough without this female's flighty influence. The Jamaican properties were too far away for the schoolteacher's condition, regrettably. The Cornwall natives were a superstitious lot; they might think Miss Lockharte's tales the work of the Devil. It would have to be Yorkshire. Neither the sheep nor their equally taciturn herders would credit her farfetched suspicions, not even if she warned them that the king of England was about to murder them all in their beds. Then again, the king of England was just as mad as Miss Lockharte.

Meanwhile, Wynn was buttoning his greatcoat around her drooping form, no easy task when she could barely hold herself erect even in the chair. Deuce take it, she needed a hat.

The female was not going to die of pneumonia, he swore to himself, not while in his care. The peagoose's cloak would have had a hood, by Jupiter. The viscount shoved his own hat on his head, stuffed his gloves in his pocket, and pulled the paisley cloth off the side table. He tossed it over her hair—no need to worry about mussing her coiffure—and tied it under her chin. He could hear Miss Merrihew sputtering in the background, so he threw a coin onto the bare table.

"There, now we are ready to go." This time Wynn opened the front door before he lifted Miss Lockharte up in his arms, greatcoat and all. Without a glance or a good-bye to the proprietress of the school, Viscount Stanford strode out to where his carriage was waiting. The driver hopped down off his perch and hurried to open the coach door.

"Go inside and make that harpy show you the way to the attic, where the rest of Miss Lockharte's things are. A cloth bag and a small lap desk. And, Tige, do shut your mouth."

While they waited for the driver's return, Wynn tried to make his companion as comfortable as possible. "I'm sorry, there is only the one pillow."

But it was clean and she was warm. Rosellen was going to be safe. She didn't know what tomorrow might bring, but for now she was out of danger. Now she could cry.

"Thunderation," Wynn swore, looking helplessly at Tige when the coachman handed in the lap desk and the satchel.

Tige just shrugged. "Don't know nothin' 'bout no weepin' fillies, m'lord. Now was she a mare, I mebbe could—"

"Spring 'em," Wynn ordered.

"Right, m'lord."

Wynn found the flask he always carried in the door's side panel. "Just the thing. Here, Miss Lockharte, this will help calm your nerves."

She looked up so that he could see those amazing aqua eyes again, swimming in tears. "No, I don't think I should. My stomach . . ."

"Will be improved by the brandy, I swear." He held the flask up to her lips and tipped it until she swallowed. He had no idea how much she took in, but she coughed, color returning to her cheeks beneath the bruises. "There, better already," he said, taking a hefty swallow for himself.

The viscount was right, Rosellen marveled as the fiery warmth spread down her chest. And she was a ninny to be weeping now that Lord Stanford had effected her escape from her attic mausoleum. She snuggled into his coat, trying not to notice the rocking movement of the carriage. It was remarkably well sprung, but her head was still spinning, even with her eyes closed. She would try not to think about it.

Instead, she replayed the viscount's dramatic rescue. No one else could have been so commanding, so authoritative. Rosellen doubted Admiral Nelson would have stood up to Miss Merrihew so bravely. Furthermore, Lord Stanford could have sent his driver back to help her, but the viscount had carried her himself in arms so strong that she hadn't felt the least frightened of the stairs. He'd wrapped her in his own coat and made sure she had her treasured possessions. He wasn't just giving her a ride to Brighton; he was giving her a new lease on life.

Why?

As the carriage rattled on, Rosellen asked herself why a gentleman of the viscount's stature would have bothered with a nobody like her. Why would he have taken her away when he could have handed her a guinea? A bit of silver should have satisfied whatever sense of duty had brought him to the school in the first place. The Merrihews would have stolen the blunt, but he couldn't have known that.

So why had he rescued her? The man was an aristocrat to his manicured fingernails, a self-important despot, as she well knew. He inconvenienced himself for no one, ignored anyone in his way, yet he had not ignored her pleas.

Why?

Rosellen snapped her eyes open to study the man in the seat across from her. He was staring out the window, impatiently drumming his fingers on his high-topped, highly polished leather boots. The noise added to the pounding in her head and she was still seeing double, which roiled her insides. The brandy was hitting her stomach now, too, with a vengeance. But she kept her eyes open, searching his countenance for answers. He was devastatingly handsome, with his dark hair fallen forward on his forehead, asking for some woman to touch it, to brush it back, just like the practiced rake he was.

The rake?

Rosellen could never pay back the debt she owed this man, not in kind, not in money. What else could he want with her? She cleared her throat and pronounced: "I will not become your mistress."

Wynn almost fell off his seat. He hadn't had that much brandy, had he? "Pardon?"

"I said I will not become your mistress, my lord."

He looked at the pathetic waif, lost in his coat, with a face that could frighten small children. He knew from holding her that a man could injure himself on her sharp bones if he got too close. And her tongue was sharper yet. And she thought . . . Wynn couldn't help himself. He laughed. And he kept laughing, slapping his knee until tears ran down his cheeks.

"My lord, please stop the carriage."

He held up his hand. "My apologies, Miss Lockharte, but the idea that you thought . . . that I would . . ." He went off into laughter again.

"Please, sir, I fear I am going to be—"

"I am sorry, truly." But he didn't stop chuckling or stop the coach.

"—sick." And she was, all over his fancy boots. Now Wynn was sorry, truly. He banged on the front panel of the carriage until it rolled to a halt.

"I'll ride ahead to make arrangements at the inn," he told

his driver. "We'll need a doctor and someone to do the nursing. Medicines, that type of thing. I'll meet you there."

"But your coat, m'lord. It's still pouring."

Viscount Stanford was halfway to Brighton.

Chapter Thirteen

$\mathscr{M}$iss Mirabel Merrihew made it a practice to know all about the ton. She knew she wouldn't let the harebrained Heatherstone twins near any of her girls. She was not being paid, and handsomely at that, to let the darling daughters of society mingle with basket-scramblers, her brother excluded, of course, being in the clergy. What Miss Merrihew did not know about the Heatherstone brothers was if they had a sister or a cousin they wished to enroll in her academy, so she agreed to see them, despite the day's perturbation. There was nothing more she could do about the Lockharte female anyway. Miss Merrihew had already put a flea in Jonas's ear and had even written to notify the school's patron, Lord Vance. Let him take responsibility for a change.

She shooed away the moonstruck maid who brought twin calling cards and frowned a herd of hovering students into retreating up the stairs, before she opened the door to the "good" parlor, the one the students never saw except on visiting days. Two equine-odored gentlemen sprang to their feet, leaving muddy footprints on her Turkish carpet. One was holding his wet hat; the other was holding what appeared to be a wet dead squirrel. At her pointed glare he stuffed the sodden pelt inside his equally sodden waistcoat.

Most people, seeing the matching redheads with their freckles and grins, were usually charmed into a smile. Miss Merrihew was not charmed and never wasted smiles on any but the most influential of customers. She was sorry, in fact, that she'd wasted her courtesies on that dreadful viscount. She was not about to look with favor on two caper-wits who rode in open carriages on rainy days. If they could not afford a coach, she could not afford the time. They had better have two sisters.

"Yes, gentlemen, what may I do for you? I am particularly busy this afternoon."

She was particularly bothered by their request to see Miss Lockharte. What could these two flash coves want with a nondescript social outcast who worked for a living? She wondered where the showy Bond Street beaux had so much as come upon the problematic miss. Miss Merrihew knew for a fact that Miss Lockharte had not received communication from them, or any other gentlemen, in the years she had been at the academy. Miss Merrihew would have read the letter first.

Even more worrisome to the headmistress was the notion that the chit was so well connected. First Stanford, now these lesser sprigs of the nobility. Miss Lockharte was even more dangerous to Miss Merrihew and her school.

Eyes narrowed to slits, Miss Merrihew asked her callers, "What did you wish to speak to Miss Lockharte about, sirs? I cannot imagine you are acquainted."

"It's personal," one of the twins answered.

"Private," the other echoed.

"I see," she said, seeing nothing but more trouble ahead. "Well, you cannot speak with Miss Lockharte, for she is gone."

"Gone?" Tom repeated, while his brother cried, "Gone? You mean we're too late? Damn, we're sunk!"

"No, we're soldiers. Sunk is in the navy. Do you feel well? Has she started haunting you yet?"

"No, but we better hurry to join up."

"But what'll we do with the kitten, bro? Can't put it back where we found it, drowning in that ditch."

"We should have brought her a dog. I told you, Tim. She didn't say anything about a cat."

"What's the difference if she's already dead?"

Miss Merrihew had had enough with gentlemen thinking Rosellen was dead when the ungrateful chit was all too lively for her own good—or anyone else's. "Sirs, Rosellen Lockharte has not passed on; she's gone off with Viscount Stanford."

"Stanford the top sawyer?" Tim asked.

"Stanford the nonesuch?" Tom asked.

"Stanford the scoundrel," Miss Merrihew replied. "The dastard drove up and carried her away without so much as a by-your-leave."

She meant the viscount had not waited for her permission; the twins assumed she meant their quarry had been abducted against her will.

Tom looked at his brother. "She ain't his type."

"She ain't no one's type," Tim responded.

"So what did he want with her?"

They both looked at Miss Merrihew, who answered, "Nothing good, you may be assured. The female was in my care and he stole her away, despite my arguments. I wouldn't be surprised if she contracts a congestion of the lungs now." She wouldn't be unhappy either.

"He stole her?"

"And she could still die?"

They looked at each other. Obviously they had to rescue Miss Lockharte.

The Heatherstone twosome left in such a hurry, Tim forgot his hat. Miss Merrihew was so angry, she stomped it flat, then kicked it into the fireplace. Good thing the twins hadn't forgotten the kitten.

They tore off, headed in the right direction by luck alone, Tim driving. "What are we going to do when we catch up to him?" his brother wanted to know.

"Steal her back, of course. Chap can't go around snatching up schoolteachers, now, can he?"

Stanford had, and Tom considered that he just mightn't be willing to give her back. "Uh, Tim, do you have a pistol?"

Tim reached under his seat and brought out a pistol.

"I better take that," the other said. "You have the reins."

"You have the kitten."

"I'm a better shot."

Tim slowed the horses. "You know, Stanford is a better shot than either of us."

Tom nodded. "He never misses at Manton's. Handy with his fives, too. Seen him working with Gentleman Jackson himself."

Tim pulled his curricle to the side of the road. "Maybe Stanford doesn't mean any harm to the female."

"He stole her, didn't he? That must mean he intends to dishonor her."

"We already did that. Stanford can't ruin her reputation if it's already gone." He set his jaw. "Someone's got to make it right."

Tom nodded. They'd discussed that beforehand. "Someone's got to marry the chit."

Both chose Stanford.

"We'll have to call him out, don't you know."

"Thought you wanted to marry his sister?" Tom shook his head. "Not good form, challenging the man about to be your brother-in-law."

Tim had to think about that. "You know, Miss Alton is a handsome woman."

"And well dowered."

"But I don't think Stanford will let me marry her anyway."

"I wouldn't, was I in charge of some innocent miss."

"That's all right then, we can challenge him." He gave the horses the office to start.

Tom was petting the kitten, inside his coat. "Ever seen the viscount fence?"

They could just make out a sleek black carriage ahead, moving up a hill. "We'll stop them at the rise," Tim said, cracking his whip over the horses' heads. "Hang on."

Before they could reach the hill, though, a single rider galloped past them. His horse was in a lather and his face was covered by a black scarf.

Both twins shouted, "Miss Lockharte!" at the same time.

Miss Lockharte was drowsing after her bout of nausea. She was getting used to the motion of the carriage or she was too tired to care. Then she heard the shouts and the pistol shot.

"Halt!" a voice called. "Or I'll shoot again!"

The coach came to a stop amid much cursing, then the door was wrenched open. A masked bandit brandished a smoking pistol, with another stuck in his waistband. "Get out," he ordered Rosellen, "or I'll shoot you where you are."

Rosellen couldn't move a finger. Besides, she had the distinct and unpleasant impression that the highwayman was going to shoot her no matter what she did. She felt sorry for the damage to the interior of his lordship's fine coach, but so be it.

"Get out, I said!"

"I . . ."

Then there was a great clamor of carriage wheels and shouting, another gunshot, horses neighing their upset. Rosellen shrank back into her corner. In less than a minute the masked bandit was gone, replaced in the doorway by two red-haired demons from her past. My word, Rosellen thought before she passed out, now she was seeing quadruple.

"Lud," Tim said, "just look at the mort. I knew Stanford was handy with his fives, but this beats the devil."

"That Merrihew female said he didn't mean any good by

her, but who would have thought the viscount would strike a woman?"

Tim stepped back from the doorway for a breath of fresh air. "Who would have thought the dirty dish kept his carriage in such a mess?"

"Uh, bro, just where is he?"

The elder Heatherstone swung around, the empty pistol making a wide circle.

Tige, the driver, was finished bandaging his arm from where the first highwayman had winged him. "His lordship is at the Blue Bottle Inn, varlets, and he's going to have both of your loose-screw hides."

"So long as he ain't here, that's aces."

"But what'll we do with her, bro?"

"Well, we can't leave her with him, that's for sure."

So they gathered up the unconscious female in a man's greatcoat and slung her onto the curricle seat, squeezed between them. Tige was reaching for his blunderbuss, so they whipped up the horses and headed for a stretch of woods they could see, following a dirt track too narrow for the Stanford traveling coach, just in case.

Rosellen was jostled awake. "What . . . ?"

"We're saving you, Miss Lockharte, that's what," one of her captors proudly announced.

The other nodded. "We rescue you from a fate worse than death, and you don't bedevil us from the grave."

"Rescue me? I was already saved by Lord Stanford."

"You was? Uh, you were? Didn't look in prime twig to us, Miss Lockharte."

"You should have seen me before," she muttered.

"And Stanford didn't, uh, get rough with you?"

"Lord Stanford was everything kind and gentle," Rosellen said, surprised to realize that it was so. "But where are you taking me?"

The twins looked at each other. They hadn't thought of that. "Can't take her to the Albany. No females permitted."

112

"Can't put her up at a hotel; pockets are to let."

"Hmm."

"Uh, Miss Lockharte, where was Stanford taking you again?"

"To the Blue Bottle Inn, on the road to Brighton."

"And he never hurt you? You wouldn't mind landing back in his care?"

Out of the rain, in a promised hot bath, away from these two imbeciles? "No," she answered fervently. "I would adore being returned to the viscount's protection."

Tim looked over her head and winked at his brother. "I smell orange blossoms, bro, don't you?"

Tom sniffed, then reached inside his waistcoat. "I smell cat piss, is what."

Wynn was waiting in the inn's courtyard, under the big blue bottle that swung from the inn's sign. The doctor had been sent for, water was heating, the innkeeper's wife was cooking a restorative broth. So where was his carriage and the blasted female? The sooner she got there, the sooner he could consign her to the landlady's care and get on about his business.

He was damp through and his boots were ruined. Deuce take it, this was the last time he was going to travel without his valet, the viscount swore. At least Jupiter was nicely bedded down in the stable, with Roger, the groom, who hadn't found any useful information.

Wynn took to pacing, a cup of mulled wine in his hand. The cup fell to the ground as his carriage tore around a corner into the yard. His prize horses were sweating and rolling their eyes; Tige's arm was bloodstained and bandaged. The driver wasn't wearing his hat either, for the thing had blown off in his mad dash after the highwaymen. It was Tige's favorite, with his initials inside, just like the nobs', but Tige Henley didn't think he'd be needing his hat; the viscount was likely to have his head.

"What the deuce happened, Tige?" Wynn shouted, rushing toward the coach.

"We was held up, m'lord. Robbed."

"In broad daylight on the king's highway to Brighton?"

"Right you are. Three of them there was, one in a mask on horseback and two redheaded devils in a curricle."

"Two . . . ?"

Tige bobbed his head up and down. "Identical, they was. Like peas in a pod."

The Heatherstone twins? Who else could it be but the brothers he was looking for? This was one coincidence too many to be halfway believable. Wynn didn't believe it for an instant. He didn't understand any of it, nor the connection to Miss Lockharte, but he'd get to that later. "What did they want?"

"The female, I s'pose, 'cause they snatched her right out of the carriage and made off with her along some goat path I couldn't follow."

"I'll kill them," Wynn swore.

Tige nodded again. "That's what I told 'em, m'lord."

Stanford was pulling open the coach door. She hadn't gone willingly, for there was her precious lap desk. He slammed the door shut and shouted for his groom. "Roger, saddle Jupiter and find my pistols."

"But I just finished—"

"Saddle him. And then help Tige clean the carriage."

The two servants were still cleaning the coach's interior half an hour later when the curricle pulled into the innyard. "It's them!" Tige yelled, grabbing up a pitchfork and running toward the curricle. Roger put his fists up, as he'd seen the toffs do at sparring practice.

"A mill!" someone shouted until the yard was filled with flailing arms.

"Where?" Tom asked excitedly before Tige reached up and dragged him out of the curricle. Tim leaped after, dropping the reins in Rosellen's lap. What she was supposed to do with them, she couldn't imagine, since one wrist was already broken and the other held a trembling kitten. If the tired horses wanted to bolt, she wasn't going to stop them. She was, however, going to stop this idiocy in the innyard so that she could have her bath. Placing the kitten on the bench beside her, she carefully reached under the seat and found the pistol Tom had reloaded. By willpower alone she managed to bring the pistol high enough to fire without shooting her own foot off. "Stop it this instant," she shouted, unheard above the din. So she pulled the trigger.

"Gor'blimey," the innkeeper swore. "She killed my blue bottle!"

Chapter Fourteen

*A*ggravation, aggravation, aggravation. That's all Baron Haverhill was getting. His gout was bothering him from the rich food, his rheumatics were bothering him from the damp weather, and having to deal with Mirabel Merrihew was bothering him most of all, from past experience. The woman made him feel as if he were back at school, trying to explain why his Latin assignment was not completed. It was not completed because Townsend Haverhill hated Latin, and he hated poker-backed, beady-eyed, skinny women with their hair scraped back and their chins thrust forward. Miss Merrihew's chin was extended about as far as it could be without jutting into the next county.

"You!" she exclaimed when the baron limped into her parlor.

He looked around. He'd sent in his card. Whom was she expecting? "Yes, well, I've, ah, come about m'niece."

"Too late by half, you are. She's gone."

"Ah, so the chit did die after all. Too bad."

"It's too bad she didn't!" It was too bad neither Jonas nor Lord Vance was having any success or suggestions. "That baggage isn't dead, and why everyone assumes she is, I'll never understand. I said she was gone, and good riddance."

"Not dead, you say?"

"Gone, run off, done a flit, taken French leave. She has turned my school upside down with her wanton ways. The students are so agitated that I shall never get them back to their lessons."

"Run off . . . Rosellen?"

"I shouldn't have taken her in, not with her spotted reputation. She was not fit company for my girls. I knew it all along. You'll hear from me, Baron, if I lose any students over this matter. I did you a favor and this is the payment I get, a scandal. And Stanford, of all people."

The woman could have been talking Latin for all the baron understood. "Viscount Stanford? What's he got to do with m'niece?"

"The libertine has *got* your niece. You figure out the rest."

Rosellen and Stanford? How was it possible the country chit knew Clarice's intended? The intentions might be all on Clarice's side, but she was a determined puss, his daughter. But Rosellen and Stanford? "The man must be a bigger rake than I considered," the baron thought out loud, "to be messing about with virgins."

Miss Merrihew's beady eyes turned to slits. "If your niece was such an innocent, why did you toss her out?"

"Quite right, quite right. Gal's no better'n she ought to be. Said so at the time." Clarice had said so, anyway, and now he believed her. In fact, he was relieved that Clarice hadn't been lying, upset that he'd distrusted her. His daughter was a Toast, while his sister's child was a trollop. This time he could wash his hands of her permanently.

Of course he didn't want to be the one to tell Clarice that her beau had run off with her dowdy cousin. Speak of agitation! Moreover, if Stanford was still in the neighborhood, Haverhill would be forced to call him out, he supposed. A gentleman had to demand satisfaction for such a slur to his family. And, damn, Stanford was a crack shot. Why did the cursed chit have to toss her cap over the windmill for such a prime goer? Aggravation, that's all Lord Haverhill foresaw.

"Don't stop until we're in Reigate," he ordered his driver. "Then take your time getting into London." Six months was what it should take for Clarice to get over Stanford. The baron pulled his hat down over his eyes and took a nap.

"They said what?" Wynn had ridden back to the Blue Bottle after three hours of trying to find a trace of the miscreants and the missing schoolteacher. He was cold, wet, and hungry, and not pleased to be met by the landlord, demanding reparations. He was less pleased to find that his groom had a black eye and his driver had a broken nose. Miss Lockharte, it seemed, had been returned soon after he left, not much the worse for wear, considering how bad was her state before. The female had most likely given the clothheads the edge of her sharp tongue, he supposed, to get her dumped back in his own lap so quickly.

The viscount was glad Miss Lockharte was safe, of course. The innkeeper's wife reported that the doctor had come and gone, satisfied with her condition. Miss Lockharte had then begged for a bath and a shampoo. Mrs. Murphy had never seen a body more bruised, nor a person rejoice in hot water more. After that, Miss Lockharte had eaten a good hot meal and gone fast asleep, which was precisely what the doctor had prescribed.

A bath, a bed, and a full belly sounded like Heaven to Wynn right now, but Tige wanted to refight his last battle.

"And you say three men abducted her, but only the Heatherstone twins returned her?"

"Right you are, m'lord, and neither of them was wearing a hat."

"What about the third man, the one with the mask?"

"The dastard had a low-crowned beaver, m'lord. But that don't mean nothing."

Wynn was willing to lay money that the third man was

Tully Hadfield, who'd left town at the same time. Tripp Hayes had also disappeared, but Hayes was a sober-minded gentleman who would never condone such a stunt. There must have been a wager or some wild dare, Wynn thought. Abducting an innocent woman out of a carriage was just the sort of mad prank the Heatherstone halfwits would pull; shooting his driver was more in line with Hadfield's brand of deviltry. And Hadfield might have figured he had a score to settle with him, after Wynn had refused his request for Susan's hand. But why pick on poor Miss Lockharte?

And then there were the final words from the Heatherpebble popinjays. "Tell me again what those clunches said," Wynn demanded of Tige.

The driver spat on the ground, to aid his concentration. "They said, m'lord, that they would do themselves the honor—them's the exact words, mind—of calling on your lordship in London, to ask your intentions toward Miss Lockharte."

How dare those two basket-scramblers question his motives? Wynn fumed. He wasn't the one who had held up a coach to drag a sick female off in the rain. "If they dare show their faces at Stanford House, I'll show them my intentions, all right. I'll bang those two heads together so hard, maybe some of the sawdust they use as brains will fall out and there will be room for a thought or two."

Tige wouldn't mind seeing the youngsters get a taste of his lordship's homebrewed, but he was duty-bound to give a full accounting. "They did make her a pretty apology, afore they left in such a hurry when the landlord reached for his rifle. He wanted them to pay for his precious bottle. Said it'd been in the fambly for generations."

"I've already paid him. That's another debt they owe."

"And they gave Miss a kitten, milord."

"A kitten?"

"You know, little furry thing with whiskers?"

"I know what a kitten is, Tige, thank you. Do you mean to

tell me they thought that would make up for the terror the poor woman must have undergone?"

"Don't know nothing about terror. She was passed out for most of the argle-bargle at the coach, then was cool as a cucumber when she had to be, when they brung her back. Never seen such shooting, and her not looking like she could lift a finger to scratch her nose. But no, the lads had the kitten aforetimes, it seems. They apologized right handsomely for that, too, said they should have brought her a dog, but this was the best they could do for now."

Wynn was wondering if his life would ever make sense again. "They knew Miss Lockharte?" Something about the kitten—no, the dog—was striking a chord in his memory. *I am dying, and I never had a dog.* Good lord, she'd written to the Heatherstone sprigs, too.

Later, after his own bath and hot meal, Wynn sat with the innkeeper's best brandy in the innkeeper's best private parlor and contemplated his best moves. The female upstairs knew the fools who'd abducted her, and now they wanted to know if he was going to do the honorable thing by her. The whole deuced coil must be nothing but a plot to get a wealthy viscount to the altar, by George! First she fed him a tale of woe until Wynn took her up, then her cavaliers came riding to her rescue, crying compromise, blast them to Hell. That was just the kind of nasty trick a dirty dish like Tully Hadfield would devise.

But could they really be thinking leg-shackles? Perhaps he was the one, now, who was seeing conspiracies in every corner.

Miss Lockharte was a schoolteacher, he told himself, like that skittish spinster back at the academy. Schoolteachers were middle-aged old maids, not marriageable misses. His sister had wanted her for a companion, and although he couldn't remember anything about the female except her unsuitability, he knew that companions were likewise not remotely in the running for a title, especially not his.

Wynn had more questions than answers. Just how old was

the woman, anyway? It had been impossible to tell, between the bruises and the pallor and the gaunt cheeks. Plot or not, she had been grievously ill.

If the Heatherstones wanted to know his intentions, they must think she was a lady, if they thought at all. Besides, they would most likely have dumped a female of less stature out on the roadway after they'd had their fun. They would never consider that Wynn should have to marry her. If she was well born, then who were her people and why weren't they caring for her? No, that wasn't a mystery, Wynn reflected, sipping his brandy. He could easily understand why her family didn't claim such a prickly female. Her other presentiments of persecution aside, Miss Lockharte was definitely dicked in the nob if she thought she could bring him up to scratch. Wynn had enough eccentric relations himself to understand how some unfortunate family could choose to let her shift for herself.

She was not, the viscount promised himself, going to shift him into parson's mousetrap.

His intentions? He was going to strangle her, that's what.

Wynn took the steps two at a time up to the bedchamber across from his. The door was slightly open, so he pushed it in, without knocking. A mobcapped maid was sleeping in a chair in the corner and a lamp was left burning. So was the fire, keeping the room as warm as a bakehouse. Wynn loosened his neckcloth as he approached the bed.

Miss Lockharte was sleeping, and not even the most righteously indignant victim of her machinations would have had the heart to awaken her. She was wearing a clean white flannel nightgown, most likely the landlady's, that buttoned at the chin, and her newly bandaged right arm lay atop the blankets, a small gray fur ball nestled in the elbow above her plastered wrist. The kitten blinked up at him with wide smoky eyes, yawned, and tucked its chin back into the folds of Miss Lockharte's nightgown. Wynn could hear its purring.

They'd washed her hair, he could see, and cut it, most likely as the most expedient way of getting rid of the tangles. The dark and dirty mop she'd had was replaced by a head of wheaten curls framing her face. Now Miss Lockharte looked like a fallen angel, Wynn thought, remembering her celestial blue eyes. The bruises were not so visible under her improved complexion, and the dirt had been washed away. Even the hollows at her cheeks were already less gaunt. She seemed to be resting peacefully, too, without the pained, pinched look he'd seen in the carriage. He glanced at the bottles and jars on the bedside table, wondering if she'd been given a sleeping draft or if she'd wake up soon so he could question her.

Wynn still couldn't tell her years. With the cap of curls, she might have been a child, except for the swelling mounds of her breasts. She was a woman, then, but her hair showed no gray and her skin seemed soft, where it wasn't swollen or discolored. She was most likely of marriageable age after all. Looking at her, though, the viscount couldn't bring himself to think of Miss Lockharte contriving a trap for his name and fortune. The poor chick was too addled, for one, too impaired, for another. No, she'd just been in the wrong place at the wrong time. For the umpteenth time, it looked like.

Chapter Fifteen

*S*omething touched Rosellen's face. "Go back to sleep, Noah," she mumbled.

Noah? Wynn's hand, which was brushing a curl off her cheek, clenched into a fist. Damn, she looked so sweet asleep, so vulnerable and needing protection, that he'd forgotten for a moment: Miss Lockharte was one of the slipperiest characters he had ever encountered, certainly the most troublesome of females. And he had known a great many troublesome females, the majority of whom did not call out men's names in their sleep. Or if they did, he did not have to know about it.

Wynn must have made some sound of disgust that he had let his imagination lend innocence to the fragile waif, for her eyes opened. They were, indeed, the eyes of an angel, which only went to prove that appearances could be deceiving. "I am sorry," he said when she blinked a few times, trying to get her bearings. "Sorry that I awakened you and sorry that I am not Noah."

Her face screwed up in confusion. "Why would you be sorry you're not a cat?"

"Noah's your cat?" Good grief, he truly was seeing goblins and ghoulies everywhere. Wynn could feel his face burning, that she might think he wanted to be in her arms like the little gray kitten. Nothing was farther from his mind, by Heaven. "You named your cat Noah?"

"He was found in a flooded ditch, it seems. Noah seemed appropriate." Her good hand was stroking the soft fur; the kitten was purring again.

"Yes, well, about this afternoon . . ."

"There's only one of you!" she exclaimed suddenly.

Oh, lud. "Yes, I know, I couldn't be in two places at once. Still, I am sorry I wasn't there to defend you. I should not have ridden off and left the coach unguarded that way."

"No, I mean that I'm not seeing double anymore! The doctor assured me the condition would improve, but you cannot imagine what a relief it is that he proved correct."

"Yes, I'm sure it was disconcerting, but—"

"To say the least. That's why I, ah, the carriage . . ."

Her voice faded to an embarrassed murmur and a blush spread across her cheeks. A maidenly blush, Wynn decided, giving further credence to the Heatherstones' presumptions. "Think nothing of it, Miss Lockharte. You were ill, and the carriage is already as good as new. You seem much improved also, which is more important."

"Thanks to Mrs. Murphy and the excellent doctor. I can never thank you enough for bringing me here, my lord. And I am sure that by tomorrow I can find a ride into Brighton to see the constable, so you need not be bothered with me any longer."

"It's no bother, I assure you."

"Nonsense, of course it is," Rosellen said in her best tutorial voice. "You have been more than kind, so you don't have to lie. I am sure you want to be off about your business, so I won't keep you."

Wynn was irked that Miss Lockharte was so positive that he wouldn't help her. The cheeky female was dismissing him out of hand, to go off on her own into Zeus knew what trouble. His mother and sister came to him with every minute dilemma, from overcharged bills to overdue lending-library books. Miss Lockharte, with less strength than her kitten, thought she could handle thieves and murderers on her own. Even if the criminals were running amok in her own mind, she should be turning to him. But she wasn't, obviously because she didn't think he had enough human kindness to inconvenience himself for a mere schoolteacher. Although that was exactly his intention, to wash his hands of her at first light, her assumption irked him. Before the Heatherstones arrived, he'd been planning to send her to one of his properties. Now he was determined to stay on and see what became of Miss Lockharte and her cohorts, see if he didn't. Besides, Wynn saw a good way of gathering the information he sought.

"Tomorrow is much too soon," he told her. "The physician said you shouldn't be moving about for a week."

"Oh, no, I have to get to Brighton long before that. I have to see about my fifty pounds so that I can repay you and Mrs. Murphy for the costs of my keep."

Did the ninnyhammer think he would take money from her, besides? Either she knew nothing about gentlemen, which was possible if she'd been associating with the Heatherstone duo, or she did not consider him one. Wynn would have slammed his fist on the nightstand if the maid hadn't been sleeping. "Mrs. Murphy has been paid. And I shall undertake your errands in Brighton. I have business there myself," he fabricated.

"Will you, truly? I don't know if it's the constable or the magistrate that I need to see to lodge a complaint about the Merrihews. I need to find Fanny also."

"Right, the missing maid who knows all about the cryptic coach and the purloined purse."

Her eyes narrowed and her hand stopped petting the kitten, who complained. "You do not believe me. You are humoring me like a fractious child."

The woman might be deluded, Wynn thought, but she was no dunce cap. "I am only looking at it from the magistrate's viewpoint. You are unclear yourself as to the money's source and the Merrihews are upstanding citizens in the community. You have no proof of your allegations."

"I have a broken wrist!"

"Yes, but you have no evidence that you did not simply lose your footing, out of weakness after the fever. No, it would be better for me to make a quiet investigation, to see if I cannot locate the maid for you first."

"I suppose that makes more sense," Rosellen reluctantly agreed. Truly she was not fit to go traipsing from door to door looking for a missing maidservant. The viscount, she supposed, could simply send one of his own retainers while he sat in some smoke-filled gaming den.

"Good. I shall need a bit more information before approaching the magistrate, in any case, such as how long you have been at the academy and where you were before. He'll want to know your bona fides. Legal types are thorough chaps, don't you know."

Rosellen actually knew very little about the law, that being another subject considered beyond a mere female's understanding. So she gave Wynn what information she could. If he was going to any trouble on her behalf, which she doubted, he deserved to know all the facts. "I was with the school for two years, before which I lived near Upper Stoughton, in Lincolnshire. My father was the vicar at St. Jerome's there before he passed on."

Warning bells were clanging in Wynn's head. A vicar's daughter? Genteelly educated to be a governess or such? That species was not bred to be the playthings of bored aristocrats.

She was going on: "That's all, except for the short time I spent with my uncle and his family in London."

He noted that she did not give a name to the loose screws who'd thrown her to the wolves this way. Merchants or shopkeepers, he supposed. Better-connected females were all too quick to puff off their consequences. "And I suppose that was where you met the Heatherstones." It was just like those numbskulls to strike up an acquaintance with cits and hangers-on.

Rosellen stared at the cat, who was trying to get the button off her sleeve. "Yes, I met them in London, briefly."

"Briefly is usually enough, with those two. It was long enough, however, for them to remember you when they decided to kidnap a defenseless female."

She glanced up to see his lowered brow. "Oh, it wasn't like that at all. They thought they were rescuing me, you see."

"From me?" Two glasses of lemonade could be chilled by the ice in Wynn's voice.

"More from the masked rider, as far as I could understand."

"Ah, yes, the third highwayman." The woman looked and sounded sincere to Wynn, as if she actually believed Hurly and Burly Heatherstone were not involved in stopping his coach and shooting his driver. Then again, she believed Reverend Merrihew had pushed her down the stairs. If she was not in on the wager, she was most definitely being used as the bait to set the trap. But a vicar's daughter fallen on hard times, what could be more of a cliché? Or more respectable?

Wynn hardened his resolve not to be caught in the snare. "And they just happened to be in the neighborhood? Doesn't that seem rather fortuitous?"

Rosellen wasn't surprised at anything anymore, not after the viscount had shown up and come to her assistance. "It seems that I wrote them letters also. While I was so ill, you know."

Viscount Stanford knew her letters all too well. "And your message sent them riding *ventre à terre* to your rescue?"

"Not precisely. The gentlemen somehow got the impression that when I died I was going to haunt them from beyond if they did not mend their ways."

"Now I wonder how those two gullible fools ever got that idea," Wynn said, noting that Miss Lockharte was having a hard time keeping her swollen lips from curving up in a smile. Little gold flecks were dancing in her eyes. He stepped back in a hurry. He had no business noticing the eyes, merry or otherwise, of a vicar's daughter.

"I am sure I cannot imagine," she said with a definite lilt, "but you can see where it would behoove them to keep me alive. They were only trying to rescue me this afternoon, I am convinced of it."

And Heaven knew what they were trying to do now: rescue her from poverty? From spinsterhood? The devil take all of them! Wynn still wasn't sure of Miss Lockharte's place in the ruse. "Tell me, what will happen if you cannot recover the blunt?"

"I could starve, I suppose." She raised her bandaged arm. "I cannot work and I have nothing to sell. Offering my body, even if I were willing to take a woman's last option, which I am not, does not seem to be an alternative, considering your reaction this afternoon." Rosellen hoped to pass off her hideous presumption as a joke.

"I am sorry, miss, I shouldn't have laughed, but I do not go around offering *carte blanche* to the victims of horse tramplings. What else will you do?"

"Quite frankly, I have been worrying myself sick over the dilemma. I suppose my only hope is to throw myself on my uncle's mercy. He didn't seem to have much of that commodity in the past, but I have no other choice." She sat up straighter, pulling the covers to her chin. "Do not think that I am looking for sympathy or handouts, my lord. You have done enough, and I do not mean to add to my debt to you. Uncle will have to provide."

"As well as he has provided in the past? Just who is this uncle who would see his own flesh and blood working for a witch like Miss Merrihew, anyway?" Wynn meant to have a word with the blackguard when he returned to London.

"Uncle Townsend is my mother's brother, Baron Haverhill."

Haverhill? The devil! Wynn rocked back on his heels, suddenly wishing the maid wasn't sleeping in the room's only chair. Then again, thank goodness the landlady's daughter was present to play propriety. Haverhill! "So that's why he was coming here," he reasoned out loud. "It was no coincidence at all. You wrote to him, too, didn't you?"

"He was coming? You relieve me. I did not want to think him so heartless." Rosellen sighed. "And if he cared enough to come for me, he will repay you, of course. I am sorry you had to go to the bother. Uncle would have helped me."

But Haverhill hadn't even shown up, Wynn thought but forbore commenting. He looked to the door to make sure it was open. Thunderation, Miss Lockharte was Clarice Haverhill's cousin!

As if reading his thoughts, Rosellen asked, "You must know Uncle if you knew his intentions. Do you know my cousin, Clarice, also? No, ignore my curiosity," she answered herself. "Of course you do. She is a Toast, after all." Clarice and this Corinthian obviously shared the rarefied ether of the elite society.

He nodded distractedly, trying without success to place a poor relation in the beauty's entourage. "But I was not in the habit of attending debutante balls and the like until my sister came to Town. I must have missed your London Season."

She laughed, but without humor. "Oh, it was no Season, more of a sennight in Hell. But I do not recall you from then either." And she would have, had the dark-haired, dashing viscount formed part of Clarice's court.

"How much older are you than Miss Haverhill?" he asked, pretending to be dredging his memory still.

She shook a fold of blanket at the kitten. "Actually, I am two years younger."

Wynn felt the sands shifting beneath his feet. Miss Lockharte was not only a vicar's daughter and a baron's niece; she was that most dangerous of manhunters, a woman of marriageable age. And here he was, in her bedroom at night in an inn, alone except for a sleeping maid. Uncle should pop in at any moment, with a loaded rifle. No wonder he hadn't fetched her out of the attics at the academy; Haverhill was waiting for bigger fish. The baron couldn't land the prize with his beautiful daughter as bait, so now he thought to use his little minnow of a niece. Damn them all to hell.

"Perhaps your uncle will arrive in the morning," he said. "I thought he was leaving town before me, but I must have been wrong." And he was wrong to be there. Wynn was in a hurry to leave, making sure his neckcloth was straight before he stepped into the hall. Lud, he was in a sweat, and not just from the heat of the room. He tried to slick his hair back with unsteady fingers. "For now, you need your rest. Good night, Miss Lockharte."

Her eyelids were already drifting closed. "Good night, Lord Stanford. And I am sorry for believing you were a pompous prig. God bless you for being a better person than I thought."

Chapter Sixteen

*R*osellen was asleep in minutes. She was comfortable and secure for the first time in forever, it seemed. Her future might be as uncertain as the weather, or as variable as a certain viscount's moods, but she was protected for now. If his lordship wished to practice his charitable inclinations on her, that was fine. She'd pay him back by disappearing as soon as she had her fifty pounds, so he wouldn't find her an embarrassment. Meanwhile, whatever else his faults, Lord Stanford would not abandon her. That is, he might leave, but Rosellen felt sure he would lend her enough money to see her through until she found her own stolen fortune or another position. Although she had doubts about his original intentions, she believed the viscount had taken her under his wing, and she was content to be there for now. Just as Noah was curled up in the space between Rosellen's shoulder and her cheek, knowing he wouldn't be hurt, so she trusted his lordship. She wasn't sure why, but there it was.

And there Wynn was, trying to sleep in his carriage. He was awake for hours. First he'd put his feet up on the seat opposite him, then he'd tried leaning sideways against the door panel. Nothing worked, but he'd be damned if he went back inside that inn. Damned to a life with a crackbrained viscountess, he'd be the laughingstock of the ton. Even his mother would rather see him remain unwed than make such a misalliance. But what to do with Miss Lockharte, that was the question keeping Wynn awake. He couldn't suffer sleeping in his carriage for a sennight and he couldn't simply walk away. There was the rub. Sending her off to Yorkshire now that he knew she was young and gently bred was no longer a viable option. The people there would immediately assume that she was his cast-off mistress. They'd treat her accordingly, making her life a misery. Even that, however, might be better than the life she'd lead as Clarice Haverhill's poor relation. Bedlam might be better. Wynn would have to make other arrangements.

He spent the next hour trying to think of anyone he knew who needed a governess or a companion. Fotheringill's children were little savages, though, and Beaumont's mother was a shrew. Wynn even considered forcing one of the hatless Heatherstones to marry her. They were the ones who'd had her unchaperoned in the open curricle, after all. No, Miss Lockharte deserved better than that, too. Hell, her kitten deserved better.

Wynn could not think of a decent alternative, but he did find a less uncomfortable position, curled on his side with his knees touching his chest. He'd be stiff in the morning, but better a sore back than a batty bride. With visions of Miss Lockharte in a white lace gown tumbling down the stairs of his mind, the viscount finally fell asleep, so he missed the fire.

Murphy woke him before dawn by opening the carriage door. The innkeeper had a grin on his face, a cup of coffee in one hand, and a purse of money in the other. He thrust the latter two at the viscount. "Here, gov'nor, 'tis the money what you gave for the blue bottle. That little gal saved my inn last night, she did. I'm thinking of renaming the place the Lucky Lady in her honor."

Lucky? Miss Lockharte? Even half asleep, Wynn knew better. Miss Lockharte was the most unfortunate female he'd ever encountered. Otherwise, he wouldn't feel so accountable for her welfare. "She isn't lucky; she just has more lives than that cat of hers. What did you say she did?"

"She saved my bacon, that's what. Put out the fire with that man of yours. I was surprised to see him there instead of your lordship, but lucky for me he was. Iffen it was yourself in the room where you was supposed to be sleeping, the bathwater wouldn't've still been in the room. But the water wouldn't've turned the trick, not without the little miss screaming loud enough to get your coachman's attention. It was the cat what first smelled smoke, too, and after my wife wanted to put the poor thing outside after supper. My, my, what a night."

Wynn had the man by the lapels of his frieze coat. Coffee and coins were both on the floor of the carriage. "What fire, by all that's holy?" he shouted. "And is Miss Lockharte injured?"

"The fire in the hall outside your room. One of the guests must have been castaway enough last night that he dropped his candle on the way to bed without even noticing. Like I said, the young lady and your man had the fire out by the time I could get up the stairs. And her with a broken wrist. My, my, I said to Mrs. Murphy, that one's a game pullet if I ever saw one. She went right back to sleep, she did. Said there was no reason to wake your lordship."

"But is she all right?" Wynn demanded.

"Better'n when she came," the innkeeper declared, but Wynn was already on his way across the inn's courtyard, headed for the stairs. "My, my," Murphy said, watching the viscount's quickly disappearing figure. "My, my."

Wynn was halfway up the stairs before he remembered he wasn't wearing a neckcloth. Hell, he wasn't even shaved. But he could smell smoke, so he kept going. Lud, these old timbers could go up like matchsticks. No wonder the landlord was grateful.

The door to Miss Lockharte's room was partially open, so

the viscount rushed right in. The female could have inhaled the noxious fumes or been burned in her bravery, despite the innkeeper's assurances. At the very least, she could be in hysterics. His mother would have had a spasm for sure; his sister would have swooned; Maude would have needed to dose herself with laudanum for a week. But Miss Lockharte, he saw when he entered the room, Miss Lockharte needed to wash her hair.

She was sitting next to the fire, with her back to him, trying to fluff her curls dry with one hand. The kitten was in her lap, batting at the towel she was ineffectively wielding.

"Here, let me do that," Wynn said, taking the towel away from her.

Rosellen licked her lips, which Wynn noted were not nearly so swollen, and glanced nervously toward the door. "I don't think you should. . . ."

"I am not trying to compromise you, miss. Trust me, that is the farthest thing from my mind. Furthermore, the door is open and Mrs. Murphy assures me that she is on her way upstairs with your breakfast."

Rosellen looked down at the borrowed robe, which enveloped her from chin to toes, twice around. Of course she did not appeal to his lordship's taste, she told herself. She was being foolishly missish again. Still uncomfortable with the presence of a man in her room, though, and a man in disarray, with a dark shadow on his jaw besides, she found herself chattering more than was her wont. "I am so glad to be rid of my long hair. This is so much easier to manage. I just had to be rid of the smell of smoke."

While he gently patted her curls, Wynn was trying to decide on their color. The soft tendrils were not an insipid blond or a common, mousy brown. They were somewhere right in the middle, he decided. Sunlight or lemon juice would make golden highlights, he was sure. His sister would know. For now it was enough that not a single hair on her head was singed. Catching himself woolgathering, he asked, "Where is the girl I hired to tend to you?"

"She was too upset to be of much use, so I sent her to her own room to rest. I am not used to having someone wait on me, anyway."

The maid was too distraught to do her job, but Miss Lockharte could calmly wash her own hair with one hand. For a female in his care to be so ill used was beyond everything Viscount Stanford believed as a gentleman. More forcefully than necessary, he demanded, "Are you sure you were not harmed in any way?"

Rosellen thought he was angry that he'd have to look after her for an extended time. She took the towel from his hand and sat back. "Quite sure, my lord, so you need not be concerned. I am sorry about your coat, however."

Wynn leaned against the mantel and watched the cat play with the tassels on his boots. "My coat?"

"Yes, the one you lent me. I hadn't had a chance to return it to you, you see, and then when Noah started meowing and I smelled the smoke, I grabbed the first thing to hand. Your greatcoat was over the back of this chair, drying. I threw it on the fire."

"What, did you dislike it so much? I was rather fond of the garment myself."

"Don't be foolish. I was trying to smother the flames before they reached the walls. The coat was still somewhat damp, thank goodness, and it contained the fire until your man Tige arrived. As soon as he saw what was toward, he went back into your room for cans of water from his bathtub. He said you were sleeping in the stables." Rosellen couldn't keep the curiosity from her voice. Gentlemen did not, in her experience, bed down with the cattle when every luxury was at their fingertips.

"I, ah, couldn't sleep, and Tige needed his rest after the harrowing day he'd spent getting held up and shot and his nose broken. We switched, is all."

"Lucky for all of us that you did," she said, once again implying that he could not have been as quick thinking or valiant as his coachman. "But I fear your coat is ruined."

He brushed that aside. "Now neither of us has a warm wrap. I am sure the Murphys will provide us with something. But tell me, Miss Lockharte, how many of me do you see?"

"Why, one, my lord. But . . ."

"Excellent. We'll set out for London as soon as we have changed and breakfasted. We'll reach town by dinnertime."

"Why ever would we do that?"

"Because you cannot wish to spend the night in yet another inn. I know I don't."

"No, I mean why would I be going to London, Lord Stanford?"

"Because you will get better care there, obviously. Susan and my mother will quite dote on you, of course, and Cousin Lenore will be good company until we can contact your Haverhill relations." Miss Lockharte would be safe, and so would he, Wynn had decided. A friend of Susan's, recuperating in town under his mother's aegis, what could be more innocent? His nerves might stop twitching.

"No."

"No, we shouldn't contact your family?"

"No, I am not going to London with you, my lord. I appreciate the honor of your invitation," she said, although he had issued a command, not an invitation, "but I cannot accept. I will not become your obligation. I am deeply enough in your debt already."

"There is no debt, Miss Lockharte, and never has been. I believe you would do better at my home than among strangers."

"I understand, my lord, that you feel you have to return to London. Please do not let concern for me stop you. Mr. Murphy said I may stay on here as long as I need. I can help him with his accounts until my uncle comes."

Wynn was pacing now, the kitten at his heels chasing the swinging tassels. "Your uncle may not come at all, Miss Lockharte. Have you considered that? He might have had a change of heart, you know, for he should have been here long ago. Or perhaps Miss Merrihew refused to give him your direction. I wouldn't put it past that harridan."

"No, I wouldn't either. I hadn't thought of that." Rosellen leaned over and scooped up the kitten, out of harm's way. His lordship looked angry enough to commit mayhem.

"Precisely!" he exclaimed. "You didn't think. I did. All night. We'll go to London and call on your uncle first thing in the morning."

"No."

Wynn was not used to being contradicted. He did not enjoy the new experience one iota. "You are trying my patience, Miss Lockharte," he said through clenched teeth, "by being difficult."

"No, I am merely disagreeing with you. There is a difference, you know."

"Thank you for that lesson, ma'am. If you are finished with your classroom lecture for the day, I'll leave you to get dressed. Please ring when you are ready to depart."

Was the man deaf or merely dense? "My lord, I shall not go to London with you. I am not budging from here until I have found my fifty pounds."

"I'll give you the blasted fifty pounds!" Wynn shouted.

"Why would you do a thing like that? You didn't steal it. And I could not accept in any case."

Wynn ran his fingers through his hair. In a minute he'd be pulling it out at the roots—or hers. Those soft brownish ringlets looked tempting. "I would give you the money to shut you up, Miss Lockharte. Damn, but you would have been better called Lockjaw! If the brass is what's keeping you from going where you'll be safe and restored to your family, then I will gladly pay the price."

"No, as I said, I am not leaving." Rosellen sat ramrod straight in her seat.

Taking a deep breath, Wynn told her, "Miss Lockharte, you

asked for my help. Now you are getting it. We are going to London, and that is final."

"No, my lord, you are going to London and I am staying at the Blue Bottle Inn."

"There is no blue bottle, thanks to you. You, miss, are a hazard."

"And that is my cross to bear, not yours. You cannot order my life, Lord Stanford. I am not your ward. I am neither in your employ nor in your keeping." She ignored his snort. "I am a grown woman who can take care of herself."

Wynn held up his right hand, ticking off each finger as he counted: "Runaway horses. Slippery stairwells. An abduction, now a fire. Did I forget anything?"

Rosellen didn't think it was a good time to remind Lord Stanford of the strangulation and suffocation attempts on her life while she was ill. "Very well, I am not doing a very good job of it at present."

"Miss Lockharte, you are making lumpfish out of living through the week!"

"That does not give you the right to order me around."

"It gives me every right. Someone has to look out for you, and I seem to be the someone in charge. Now you can come with me politely or I can carry you down the stairs. No, I'll likely end up carrying you anyway," he said, looking at her pale face and trembling lip, "so it makes no matter what you do."

"You never did intend to find Fanny for me, did you?"

Blast, those azure eyes were filling with tears again. "Yes, I did. And I intend to leave Roger behind to make inquiries. Will that satisfy you?"

"No, do you care?"

"Stubborn wench, I care about getting you locked up someplace safe so I can get my sanity back!"

"If I am such a burden," she said with a sniff, "why are you bothering with me?"

"Miss Lockharte, all women are burdens. You, at least, are interesting."

"But not interesting enough for you to respect my wishes."

"I respect your wishes, miss. I simply do not agree with them. There is a difference, you know," he said, throwing her words back at her.

Rosellen dabbed at her eyes with the towel. "Do you recall my apology of last night, when I said I was sorry for calling you a pompous prig?"

He nodded, handing over his handkerchief.

"Well, I take it back."

Chapter Seventeen

They set out for London after lunch. Rosellen insisted on waiting to see if her uncle arrived; he did not. Defeated, she agreed to leave. Her agreement, of course, was simply a matter of pride since the viscount was not giving her a choice. She left Noah with Mrs. Murphy, who begged to keep the hero of the inn. Rosellen was uncomfortable enough going to Lord Stanford's home herself, much less bringing a kitten along, and if she did end up at her uncle's, poor Noah would be relegated to the kitchens, if not the backyard. Aunt Haverhill was cat-feverish. The cat would be better off guarding the Blue Bottle from fire, but now Rosellen had another gripe against his lordship. She decided not to speak to him, to show him what she thought of his domineering manner. Her resolve was easy to keep, since she sat inside the traveling coach with Letty, Mrs. Murphy's daughter-in-law, and Wynn sat outside on the driver's bench with Tige. He wanted to give her privacy, the viscount claimed. More likely he didn't want to give her the chance to express an opinion of the scenery, Rosellen believed. She'd never met a more high-handed, autocratic despot in her life.

On the other hand, she had to admit, he had arranged for her to have a female companion on the journey and he had provided her with a warm cape. Most important, he had left his groom behind to find Fanny. How could one person be so kind and yet so cloddish? Rosellen did not have an answer. Letty wanted only to talk about what a fine figure of a man he was. Didn't Miss think so? Rosellen still didn't have an answer, so she decided to take a nap.

At one of the changes, Wynn ordered tea in the inn's private parlor. When he noticed how uncommunicative his guest was, he asked if she was feeling poorly. They could rest there the night, if she'd rather. Rosellen would rather return to Brighton. Then he decided she was simply anxious about her welcome at Stanford House.

"There is nothing to worry about, you know. Susan will be in alt to have you with her. She quite sings your praises. My mother will be delighted if you help keep Susan occupied, and Cousin Lenore won't mind in the least taking another young lady about with her."

Rosellen was so startled, she forgot her vow of silence. "Taking another young lady about with her where?"

"Why, to all the parties and balls, of course." He made a grimace in the direction of her shapeless gray uniform, which was as clean as Mrs. Murphy could get it. "Shopping, too, I daresay, as soon as you are feeling up to it."

"In case you've forgotten, I have no funds to go shopping, my lord."

"I did remember, Miss Lockharte. How could I forget with you giving Roger reams of instructions for the recovery of your fifty pounds? And I did guess that you would fly up in the boughs over it, so I decided I would make you a loan until you recover your own funds. If, that is, your uncle does not claim you for the Season."

"The Season? My lord, you are talking fustian. I do not need your loan, for I do not need a new wardrobe, for I won't be attending any of those entertainments you mentioned. I am no debutante making her curtsy to the crown, no belle of the *belle monde*."

"But you do deserve to have some fun," he insisted, peeling an apple for her.

"Those of us who work for a living do not have 'fun,' my lord. It is not in our contracts. I am not a member of your pleasure-seeking, sophisticated society, nor do I wish to be."

"But you *will* be. There is no other way for you to meet eligible young gentlemen."

"No, thank goodness, I won't be forced to meet the likes of the Honorable Heatherstones or their friend who died. Incidentally, I did not kill him."

Confound it, Wynn thought, just when the female was making rational conversation—pigheaded and persnickety, but rational—she tossed in a bizarre statement that was going to make his job of getting her married off all the harder. "I never assumed you did, my dear. Ah, while we're at it, did you ever happen to meet Tulliver Hadfield when you were in London?"

"No, not that I recall. Why?"

"Just that he's the type you do not want to know. What about Tripp Hayes?"

Rosellen shook her head. "You can list a hundred names, my lord, but I met very few gentlemen, and fewer who deserved the title. I will not be going back into their midst."

"Of course you will. How else can you find the one to marry? And no, don't say you don't wish it. All females wish to be married." And he wished to see her wed, that being the best solution he'd arrived at for the disposal of Miss Lockharte.

Rosellen laughed. "Once again my wishes do not enter into the equation. Even if I wanted to find a husband, I have no dowry and my own family has cast me off for all intents and purposes. I do not have looks or flirtatious ways." Rosellen remembered that she could not attract so much as a dishonorable proposal from one of London's premier womanizers. "And I left London under a cloud two years ago. No, sir, I do not think I would fare well on the marriage market."

"Gammon. I suspect you'll be a handsome female when you get your health back, and not every gentleman needs a wife to fill his coffers, besides his bed. As for gossip, the ton has a short memory. There have been a thousand scandals worse than yours, whatever it was. Finally, you will be sailing under my mother's flag. No one would dare snub you."

"They won't, because I am never stepping one foot into their circles and that's final."

"Never say never, Miss Lockharte. Nothing is final except death."

Rosellen thought back to the night she believed she was dying. Sometimes not even death was all that final.

They arrived well past dinnertime, and the ladies of the house were out, the butler informed Lord Stanford. Wilkins looked past his employer, ignoring the drooping, draggletailed female on his arm.

"Miss Lockharte will be staying? Very good, milord."

His sniff told a weary Rosellen that the starched-up butler did not think it was a very good idea at all. She did not like the way he asked, "Which bedroom shall I have Mrs. Wilkins give her?" either, as if the majordomo were assuming Wynn would say his own. She half expected the viscount to say the attic, she had been so troublesome to him. She tried to stand straighter, without his lordship's support.

In the end she was half carried up the marble stairwell by Wynn himself to a suite of rooms next to Susan's, with two maids assigned to help her. Wilkins bowed himself out with the utmost deference. If that was the way the wind was blowing . . .

Rosellen was asleep almost before the maids left the bedchamber, too tired to notice her surroundings except for the bed, which was the softest she'd ever slept in, and the pillow, which smelled of lavender.

Wynn returned below, after giving instructions for Letty Murphy's care and transport back to the Blue Bottle in the morning. He went through some of his correspondence while waiting for his family to return. He wanted to speak with Stubbing, too, their escort, according to Wilkins. At least the lieutenant was good for something, Wynn thought, eyeing the haphazard piles of papers on his office desk, for the fellow was not much of a secretary.

Before long he heard Wilkins welcome the party home, so he went to greet them in the hall and help the footmen carry his mother and her Bath chair into the parlor. "And a moment with you later if I might, Stubbing?"

"Of c-course, sir," the lieutenant stuttered, blushing a fiery red and fleeing as if he were afraid of being called on the carpet or sent to another poetry reading.

Wynn shrugged. He'd deal with the military later. "Where is Cousin Lenore? I wanted to speak with all of you at once. If I'd known she was at home I'd have asked her to look in on Miss Lockharte."

"Oh, Wynn, you brought her home with you!" His sister stood on tiptoe and kissed his cheek. "How wonderful! And she didn't die!"

"To everyone's surprise, it seems, no."

"Then I'll just run up and welcome her—"

"No, Sukey, don't go up. She's sleeping. The poor puss has had a sorry time of it, I fear. You'll have to wait until morning."

Susan turned to her mother. "You remember my speaking to you and Lieutenant Stubbing about Miss Lockharte, Mama? She is the young lady I wished to hire as my companion."

"Perfect timing then," the viscountess said, opening the workbasket Wilkins placed in front of her wheeled chair after he brought in a tea tray. "Now I won't have to haul my aching bones to another harp recital."

Wynn accepted a cup of tea. He was still chilled after riding in a thin wool coat on the carriage box all evening with Tige.

"Is Cousin Lenore ill then?" Nothing else would have gotten his mother to exert herself except a high-stakes card game.

"The chit had to return home on some business with her in-laws. I thought they didn't want her, which is why she came to stay with us." Lady Stanford was miffed all over again. She signaled Wilkins to pour her a sherry instead of the tea while she sorted through her threads. "Her note did not say when she'd be back, but she took most of her things. Ungrateful wench, I'd say."

Susan was nibbling on a macaroon. "But it is no matter now, Mama, since Miss Lockharte is here. She can go about with me."

Wynn disagreed. "First, she needs time to recover. And second, she is still not a fit chaperone for you, Sukey."

"What, is she not a lady then?" his mother wanted to know. "Why in Heaven's name did you bring her here?"

"She is too a lady," Susan insisted, instantly coming to her friend's defense. "Her father was a vicar and she has titled relations. Besides, she is everything polite and well mannered."

Wynn wasn't so sure about "polite and well mannered," after the icy treatment he'd received all day and not from the chill breeze atop the carriage. Still, he held up his hand. "Hold, brat, I did not mean Miss Lockharte was not gently bred or behaved. She is simply too young to be a proper chaperone." He looked toward his mother. "The female is younger than Sukey. Furthermore, she's been desperately ill. I am afraid she has not quite recovered in her body or her mind."

"Skitter-witted, is she?" the viscountess asked. "Fevers can do that. I recall Uncle Fred coming down with a quincy. He was never the same after—"

"No," Susan protested. "Miss Lockharte is the most level-headed, reliable person."

Wynn sipped his tea. "She is deuced peculiar, Susan, and that's a fact."

Lady Stanford shrugged that off. "Lots of eccentrics in the ton. The gal will fit right in. Be good company for Susan, at any rate. And if Miss Lockharte cannot play propriety, Stanford, you'll have to watch out for both of them, that's all. I am too weary. A gel doesn't need a chaperone if she's got her own brother as escort and a lady friend along."

"I will not go to those insipid debutante balls and picnics, Mother."

The viscountess pushed her embroidery back into its basket and started to wheel her chair toward the door. "Fine. In that case I am sure Miss Lockharte will be happy to sit at home with Susan and me until Lenore gets back, if the chit does return to us at all. Susan's little schoolteacher friend cannot be used to having gay times at that academy, can she? She won't realize what she's missing. Does she embroider, do you know?"

"Stubbing!" Wynn called. "Get in here!"

Susan gave the young man a smile that set the lieutenant to blushing again, Wynn noted as he bade his mother and sister good night. "Don't let the minx plague you, Stubbing," he advised.

"Oh, no, sir, Miss Susan would never do that."

"Hah! But tell me, did Whitehall come up with any new leads? Have you any information for me?"

Wynn wasn't surprised when the lieutenant had to admit that they were no further along in their investigation than before Lord Stanford had left.

"Well, we can eliminate Lord Haverhill and the Heatherstone halflings from our list of suspects. They were all out of town on the same errand. I am afraid we'll have to keep Tripp Hayes under investigation. The man just wasn't where he was supposed to be. I cannot imagine why my old friend would have his man lie to me. And Hadfield never showed up either, you say? That one bears watching. But, meantime, do you think you might look into the background of a pair of Sussex citizens? They are Reverend Merrihew and his sister, Mirabel. There is something deuced havey-cavey about that twosome."

Stubbing wrote the names down on a pad. "Do you think they could be the French contacts?"

"What, smuggling toy soldiers? No, they are more likely liable to commit larceny, if that. They are certainly guilty of producing young females as empty-headed as possible."

"Miss Lockharte, sir?"

"No, that one's head is too full of wild imaginings. I was thinking of my sister, Stubbing, and that smile she gave you. A word to the wise: Unless I miss my guess, the minx has matchmaking on her mind."

"She d-does?"

"Yes, I can recognize that look at a hundred yards. She inherited it from my mother, you know. But it won't do, Stubbing."

The color was flowing and ebbing on the poor lieutenant's face, first a blush, then a blanch. "It-it w-won't? That is, I know, sir."

"Yes, Miss Lockharte is not suitable for a diplomat's wife. She has a stubborn streak so wide it wouldn't fit through the doors of Lord Castlereagh's dining room. And she's too outspoken by half."

"Miss Lockharte?"

Chapter Eighteen

"Hell and confound it, that female is as hard to kill as a tick on a tiger's tail. What will we do now?"

"I am thinking. One of us has to."

"The bailiffs haven't appeared. Maybe she won't talk."

"And maybe pigs can fly. It's a sure bet that if they can, you'll never get to eat bacon again."

"Well, you were the one who said no one would believe an attics-to-let female like her."

"No one hereabouts. But if the wench has Stanford in her pocket, we're ditched. A woman can get a man to believe anything when he's in rut."

"You never got Vance to believe he ought to leave that dry stick he's married to," Miss Merrihew's loving brother noted. "Besides, Stanford cannot be panting after the Lockharte female. You saw her, Mirabel."

"And I saw you trying to corner her in the choir loft. If you ever managed to keep your pants buttoned, we wouldn't be in half this mess. There's nothing for it, you'll have to go to London to find out where he's stashed the girl. Every hackney driver is bound to know where Stanford keeps his *chères amies*."

The reverend was not averse to a jaunt to the capital. His finances rarely afforded such an expense, but if his sister was paying . . .

Miss Merrihew was thinking. "Yes, you'll go up to London. What could be more natural than the academy's spiritual adviser calling on some of its former students to find out how they go on? You'll drop a hint or two about poor Miss Lockharte's fall from grace and how the viscount took advantage of her confused and deluded state. You'll be all concern for the welfare of her health, her mind, and her immortal soul. Then you'll kill her. Try to make it look like a suicide this time, you clunch."

Rosellen awoke with a start, almost as if someone had walked over her grave. But she was very much alive, and in a lovely room with sprigs of lavender painted on the silk wallpaper. A fresh bouquet of the flowers was on the bedside table next to her and the fire was already lit. Rosellen would have pinched herself, except she did not need any more black-and-blue marks. She was actually at Stanford House. She did not know why the viscount had been so insistent, or how long she would stay, but she did not intend to waste a moment of her time there lolling about in bed. After she'd come so close to losing it, life seemed more precious than ever.

She was used to getting up early, and had done nothing but sleep for weeks, it seemed. Now she wanted to be up and accomplishing. Unfortunately, the ormolu clock on the mantel read six o'clock. Londoners did *not* get up at the crack of dawn; Rosellen knew that from her last visit. Still, she could get washed and dressed and see if she could find the kitchens for a cup of chocolate.

First she had to find her gown. None of her gray uniforms was hanging in the clothespress or folded in the drawers. Her satchel was missing altogether, although her mother's lap desk was on a table in the sitting room. Was she a prisoner then, to be kept in a violet-scented cell? Not even the overbearing Wynn Alton would dare do such a thing. Or would he?

Rosellen was about to go and give the viscount a piece of her mind, near dawn and her flannel nightgown notwithstanding, when a young maid entered the room, a pile of pastel-colored gowns draped over one of her arms. She seemed more surprised to find Rosellen awake than Rosellen was to see her.

"I'm sorry I didn't hear the bell, miss. I was just pressing these gowns for you to choose from. I would have brought a pot of chocolate."

"That's quite all right. I didn't ring, and I can find my way downstairs."

The girl—Betsy, she informed Rosellen—looked uncertain. "The ladies never take breakfast except in their rooms, miss. But Mr. Wilkins did say you were to have whatever you wanted."

"Fine, I want my gowns returned."

Betsy looked at the dresses in her arms, then at the frayed cuffs on Rosellen's nightgown. "Whatever for, miss? Miss Susan picked these out special for you until you can have new things made. I'm to take in seams or let down hems as need be."

"I cannot wear Susan's clothes!"

"Pardon, miss, but these are her last year's clothes, and I'm afraid her feelings will be hurt an you don't accept. Besides, it wouldn't do for Miss Susan's friend to look a fright when morning callers come, would it?"

Rosellen's past was embarrassment enough. She could not repay the viscount's kindness by looking like a peasant in his parlor. And the dress Betsy was holding up was silk, shell-pink silk.

"Here now, miss, you can't be a-weeping in a silk gown, else you'll have stains. If you don't like the gown, we can try another."

Betsy did not consider her dressed until the bodice of the gown was taken in to fit Miss Lockharte's fever-thin frame.

"I would gain weight, I'm sure," Rosellen said, her stomach protesting the delay until breakfast, "if I could just go down to the kitchens."

But Betsy thought she needed a matching ribbon in her hair, with the curls trimmed more evenly. Then she required a madras shawl to use as a sling for her bandaged arm, a touch of the hare's foot to cover the remaining bruises, and a tiny dab of color on her cheeks. "Just so's it doesn't look like the Altons are neglecting one of their guests. And, miss, company does not visit the kitchens. Cook would up and quit, I swear."

Wynn swore under his breath, that his solitary meal was being interrupted by the prickly Miss Lockharte. He was trying to decide what was best for her and did not need her interference. He was going over the eligible bachelors in his mind, wondering which could handle a short-sheeted shrew. Then he got a better look at his uninvited breakfast partner and swore again. Deuce take it, the female could be stunning with a few more pounds on her and a few less frowns. His task just got easier. The schoolteacher looked well rested, he noted, and most of the injuries were healed or hidden. Even her lips looked less swollen and more, well, kissed. Well kissed, Wynn amended, then caught himself. He had no business noticing Miss Lockharte's lips, and certainly not in the same sentence with kissing.

He held her seat, then gestured for a footman to fill a plate for her from the sideboard.

"Two pieces of toast and jam would be heavenly," Rosellen told the footman, who, looking over at his employer, piled a selection of eggs and bacon, kippers and kidneys on the plate. Then he went back for another plate, for the toast and jam.

"But I could never—"

Wynn waved the footman out of the room before she could protest more. Didn't the plaguey chit ever know what was good for her? "I see Susan found something for you to wear," he commented, hoping she would shut up and eat.

Rosellen touched the silky skirt. "Yes, but only until I can purchase my own." She was wondering how far her fifty pounds would go. In the country, the sum was a fortune. In London, she worried that it mightn't buy her enough time to plan a future. "Or perhaps I'd do better to make my own gowns. I know there are places where one can purchase slightly damaged dress lengths."

If her sacklike uniforms were an indication of Miss Lockharte's skill with a needle, Wynn did not want to see the results, nor did he want to see her dressed in a costermonger's castoffs, not if his ambitions for her were to succeed. "No, the modistes work for pennies," he lied. "Do you need me to cut your meat?"

"I do mean to pay you back for all the expenses, so I hope you are keeping account."

"My secretary will take care of it," Wynn offered, wondering if Stubbing would recognize a ledger book if he saw one. "Have a sweet roll. The butter is made at Alton Abbey, from our own milch cows."

Rosellen held firm. "I will not accept charity, my lord."

He pushed the jar of honey toward her. "So you've mentioned many times. Would you accept a position then?"

Rosellen put down her cup of tea. "As what?"

Wynn wished the chit would stop seeing conspiracies behind the coffee urn. Here she was looking so winsome that he almost forgot she had windmills in her attic. "As companion to my mother and Susan, of course. Cousin Lenore was called home, wherever that may be. Do try some of Cook's pudding."

"I'm sure it's delicious," she said without tasting it. "Are you serious, my lord, that you would really employ me?"

"Not as a chaperone for my sister. You are still too young and . . ."

"Unprepossessing? Unconnected? Unpolished?"

"Unfledged yourself. I much prefer to have you stay on as our guest if you do not move directly to your uncle's, but, yes,

I would hire you as a companion to my mother and sister rather than have you seek a position elsewhere."

"A position," she said, sighing, absently chewing on the toast he had spread with jam. Rosellen would have nibbled on his neckcloth if he'd handed it to her, she was so elated. A position, she said to herself. Where she wouldn't have to live in the attic or fear for her life. She'd have wages of her own and a bed of her own. She did not expect to keep the lavender suite, but the meanest room in Stanford House had to be better than anything at Miss Merrihew's.

The viscount was going on, thinking her silence was a rejection. "No one needs to know of our arrangement, of course. I would not have you treated as second class by Susan's friends or the servants. And you'll have to dress the part, naturally. A wardrobe would be included with your remuneration." He pushed another piece of toast, dripping jam, at her. "It's customary in these arrangements." His mother had paid for Lenore's dressing, he knew, so that wasn't an outrageous taradiddle.

"What about Susan? I'll have to confer with her, to see if she still wants me."

Susan had no choice, but Wynn did not wish to get into another argument about the right of women to order their own lives. "We discussed it last night and Susan is thrilled. She already has you paired with Lieutenant Stubbing, my secretary."

Rosellen laughed, the gayest, most natural laugh Wynn had heard from her. Now the viscount had two missions: to get Miss Lockharte fired off into a comfortable marriage and to make her laugh again.

"Susan always did have the most romantical imagination. I'm sure your secretary is safe from my coils."

Wynn wasn't so sure, hearing that sweet sound. "And my mother is delighted that she won't have to attend any more musicales, so there is nothing to fear except that your uncle might have prior claim to your company." Wynn had plans there, too, but until he spoke to Haverhill, he would not mention them to Miss Lockharte.

Rosellen had forgotten all about her uncle. How could she tell Lord Stanford that she'd rather stay on as a pampered upper servant than return to her own kin as an unpaid, unloved lackey? Susan would get married, but Lady Stanford would always require someone to fetch her sewing or read to her or handle her correspondence. Rosellen would be needed. She could even be governess to Susan's children or his lordship's. What an odd notion that was, to be sure. She would not take time now to consider why the notion of Lord Stanford's offspring should be unpleasant. He only wished her to be company for his sister. On the other hand, if her uncle had gone to the academy looking for her, perhaps he did care, after all. Family of one's own was a precious thing, too.

"Yes, the sooner I speak to my uncle, the better."

"I thought I'd find him at one of his clubs today." Wynn tried not to put too much emphasis on the *I*, although he did have hopes of conducting his business with the baron without Miss Lockharte's presence.

"No, Uncle Townsend would not have left Haverhill House yet. He rarely departed before my aunt and cousin were abroad." But he used to disappear shortly thereafter. "There is time to catch him at home, for the ladies are never seen downstairs before noon. I think a morning call would be better than waiting for the afternoon, when my cousin and aunt will be entertaining. What do you think?"

Stanford thought she wanted to avoid those impossible females as much as he did. Thank goodness for small favors. Wynn made one more futile try. "Since this is nearly your first day out of the sickroom, though, don't you think you should return upstairs for a rest, Miss Lockharte? Unless you're not through eating, of course." She had not eaten anything but the two pieces of toast and jam she'd ordered, dash it. How was he going to get her fired off when she looked as if the first breeze could blow her away? "And Susan will be stirring soon. You can share another breakfast with her, that's the ticket."

"I could not rest easy until I've spoken to my uncle. The uncertainty, don't you know."

"I'd be happy to tell you what he said as soon as—"

"You're right, my lord, both of us do not need to go. I am sure you have better things to occupy your morning."

"I am going. You should stay here."

"What, and let you and my uncle decide my fate between you?"

Who better? Wynn thought. A chit with bats in her belfry?

Chapter Nineteen

The baron did not know whether to call for a preacher, a pistol, or a passage to the Colonies. "Stanford's here with m'niece, you say?" He inched away from the silver salver his butler held out, as if the engraved calling card upon it had just sprouted fangs and scales. He chose to be offended. "How dare the dastard bring his damaged goods here, after he's ruined her. Neither one is fit for decent company. Show Stanford and his fancy piece the door, Jamison, else I'll be forced to call the blackguard out."

"Very good, milord. But they did arrive in the dowager viscountess's open landau."

"You saw the crest, eh?"

"And the raised platform for Lady Stanford's wheeled chair."

"And the dowager is in Town. Saw her m'self last night at that blasted poetry reading. So the Lockharte chit must be staying at Stanford House. Damn, who would have believed he'd take his ladybird to his mother's?"

The butler coughed. "Miss is dressed as a lady of fashion, milord, not as a lady of the night. And a highly respectable abigail is riding with them."

"What are you trying to say, man, that he didn't dishonor m'niece by stealing her away from her employer?"

"I am sure I could not say, milord, but he does seem to be treating Miss Lockharte with all due courtesy. Perhaps he has come to make formal application for the young lady's hand?" And wouldn't that just set the cat among the pigeons here at Haverhill House? Jamison would be delighted to see Miss Clarice taken down a peg or two, with her country cousin making the match of the Season.

"Hmm. I suppose I could demand he do the right thing, if he's not coming up to scratch on his own. You'd better show them in."

Rosellen was looking as pretty as a picture, the baron thought, except for the sling around her neck. "Deuce take it, Rosellen, I knew you weren't at death's door," he said when they were seated. "I made that cursed trip to Worthing for nothing. Aggravated my rheumatism, it did. You should have waited."

"I was ill, Uncle. I don't know what would have happened to me if his lordship had not come along and offered me a ride to the nearest inn."

"An inn, eh?" The baron was still hopeful.

"Where the innkeeper's wife watched over her like a mother hen with one chick," Wynn put in, making sure Haverhill knew his niece had not gone unattended. He did not mention the Heatherstones or their abduction; the baron already had a certain glint in his eye. Wynn took his quizzing glass out and polished it, the better to stare him down with. "Miss Lockharte's situation was dire, Baron. She could not stay at the academy, where no one was caring for her."

"Not caring for me?" Rosellen squawked. "They were trying to—"

The viscount hurried on: "If I had known you would arrive eventually, however, I would have waited and let you escort Miss Lockharte back to London. She should have had family with her, not the landlady's daughter-in-law." In one breath he managed to put the baron in the wrong for not coming sooner to his niece's rescue and himself out of the race for the altar.

"Quite, quite. But that Merrihew female only told me you'd gone off with Stanford, puss. Where was I to look?"

Or what was he to think? Rosellen also mistrusted her uncle's calculating scrutiny of the viscount. The girls at the school would have called Wynn bang up to the mark, in his fawn pantaloons and burgundy superfine coat. Uncle would like to call him nephew-in-law, it seemed. How ridiculous! Wynn was a nonpareil and Rosellen was a nobody. He owed her nothing while she just happened to owe him her very life. She could not, therefore, see him repaid with such allegations as Uncle Townsend was insinuating. Rosellen just hoped her relative would not embarrass them all. "His lordship has been everything courteous and kind, Uncle."

The baron was annoyed. Here was a philanderer of the first water. Why, in all of England, did he have to play propriety with this one silly female? If the viscount didn't take the chit off his hands, Haverhill would be stuck with her. "Then he should have brought you directly here, so there could be no tittle-tattle."

Now Wynn did look at the older man through his quizzing glass, as if he were studying a bug that had crawled out from beneath a rock. "It was late. Miss Lockharte was exhausted. I placed her in my mother's care. Who is going to gossip?"

Rosellen saw that her uncle was getting red in the face. "You do not need to worry, Uncle. Lord Stanford has offered—"

"Yes?" The baron sat forward eagerly.

"I have offered her the hospitality of my home," Wynn put in smoothly. "My sister is lonely for a young woman her own age and my mother's condition does not permit her to get around as much as she might wish. Miss Lockharte would be welcome for as long as she wishes to stay."

Haverhill almost fell off his chair, this time in relief. "That might be for the best. My wife is subject to 'conditions' of her own and couldn't help the injured chit." He did not say that his spouse could not nurse a cold or that his daughter would not tolerate comely competition. Besides, who knew what would happen with the girl under Stanford's roof? If she worked at it, she might get compromised after all. "What do you say, puss, would you like to visit with the dowager awhile? There's no gainsaying she's a high stickler, so your reputation won't be in question."

"I'd like it above all things, Uncle."

"There, that's settled. I'll give your aunt and Clarice your direction. I am certain they'll be calling on you soon."

So was Wynn. The baron's ambitious daughter wouldn't lose the chance to try to fix his interest. If he had to suffer, Wynn thought, so should Haverhill. "I didn't wish to discuss this in Miss Lockharte's presence," he said with a frown in her direction. "But your niece will need a new wardrobe. My sister is out and about constantly, and I'm sure you'd want your niece dressed appropriately."

A wardrobe was a cheap enough price to pay if it kept Rosellen away from his Clarice. Damn, when had the chit grown so pretty? If she'd been this attractive two years ago, he'd have insisted she stay on and snare a husband. Now, escorted by a top drawer like Stanford, accompanied by his sister and mother, she was bound to catch some gentleman's eye. "Of course she has to dress for her station. You may send the bills to me as long as you do not land us all in the poorhouse, Rosellen."

"And a bit of pin money, Baron? You wouldn't wish your niece to be unable to pay for her own thread and books and bonnet trims. I could lay out the funds, of course, but then the rumor mill would get to grinding about Miss Lockharte's virtue. You wouldn't want that, I am sure."

"Incidental money, of course. I should have thought of it." Haverhill rang for the butler, then whispered in the man's ear. Jamison disappeared, only to come back with a small purse, which he placed on Rosellen's lap with a stiff bow.

Satisfied, Wynn stood to go, offering Miss Lockharte his

arm. "Oh, one last thing, Baron. If an eligible suitor should approach me about paying his addresses to your niece, I may refer him to you concerning her dowry, may I not?" He raised one dark eyebrow.

A dowry? Haverhill was having to spring for another closetful of clothes and now he was expected to produce a dowry for his wayward ward? Next thing he knew, Stanford would be dictating terms. But how could he refuse when this top-of-the-trees nobleman was making a veiled threat to tell the world that Townsend Haverhill was a nipcheese? Lady Stanford could see that the doors of Society were closed to Clarice if the dowager thought her houseguest was being slighted. By Jupiter, then Haverhill would have both chits on his hands forever! The baron nodded, jowls flapping, and showed his unwelcome and expensive guests to the door before the wily viscount could think of another way to spend someone else's money.

Rosellen was awed. "That was masterful, my lord," she said to Wynn when they were back in the carriage. "You have missed your calling."

He didn't pretend to false modesty. "I always thought I could do well in the diplomatic corps."

"No, I meant you could have found a vocation as a horse trader. Why, in another minute you might have talked my uncle into purchasing me a carriage of my own!"

"Haverhill must have thought so, too, the way he hurried us out the door." Wynn barely had time to ask about the baron's hat.

"The results were everything I could have wished, but I still say that your high-handed method was abominable. But I don't mean to pull brass tacks with you, my lord, for you have given me a future!"

"And not as a paid companion, so you can stop 'my lording' me. Stanford will do if you cannot bring yourself to call me Wynn."

"Not as a servant, Stanford," she agreed happily. "And please call me Rosellen. That way I might come to believe that

I am really not a schoolteacher anymore. But I might still ask your mother for references if I cannot find a gentleman to marry. I won't wed simply anyone, you know."

Wynn was not surprised to hear that the chit planned on being as pigheaded about that decision as about every other suggestion he'd made. He sighed, wondering how long it would take to get her fired off properly. "Until the paragon who meets with your approval happens by, please consider yourself a welcome guest."

"Thank you, for I doubt even your smooth tongue could get Uncle to pay for an establishment of my own. But I do not understand."

"It is just not done, Miss—ah, Rosellen. Young ladies do not live alone without incurring just the kinds of reputations we have been at pains to avoid."

"No, I do not understand why you have been so kind to me."

Wynn glanced to where the maid was pretending an interest in the passing traffic. He could not say that Miss Lockharte's scathing deathbed letter had hurt him or that her sad plight had moved him. He couldn't admit that he wanted this determined little dragoness to like him, not aloud and not to himself. "Perhaps I merely wish to see justice done."

Rosellen wasn't entirely convinced, but the maid's presence kept her from pursuing the altogether too fascinating study of the workings of Wynn Alton's mind. "In that case, could we stop by Bow Street, because I wish to hire a Runner with the purse Uncle gave me."

"Great gods, a respectable female doesn't call at Bow Street, where criminals are constantly paraded through the doors. Why would you wish to hire a Runner, anyway?"

"Why, to start an investigation into the Merrihews' conduct and to recover my stolen money, of course."

Wynn was almost shouting, and the maid be damned: "Are you still riding that hobbyhorse? Confound it, you have money of your own now, enough for a wardrobe and whatever else you might need. You have the opportunity for a family of your own, or a position if your uncle comes the crab. Why the devil would you want to jeopardize all of that?"

"Perhaps because I, too, wish to see justice done, my lord."

The informal luncheon was a cheerful affair, now that Rosellen's immediate future was decided. Wynn kept urging dishes on her, and Susan kept thinking of places her friend would like to visit, sights she would want to see, shops she absolutely had to patronize. Lady Stanford was happy that she didn't have to go along with them to Astley's Amphitheatre, Ackerman's Repository, or the animal menagerie at the Tower. Red-faced, Lieutenant Stubbing allowed as how he'd be delighted to escort the ladies wherever they wished to go, anything to avoid his lordship's ledgers.

Lord Hume was in a good mood, too, pleased to make Miss Lockharte's acquaintance over the turbot in oyster sauce, after his talk with Wynn. There was no news about his hat, but neither was there an extortion note or a mention in the *on dits* columns of the journals. Hume was beginning to agree with the viscount that the loss of his top hat and his cherished *billet-doux* was a mere misfortune, not a dire calamity.

And Wynn was glad to see how well Rosellen fit in with his household. At least she was no odder than the others. She didn't blush or babble and never spoke of Bow Street, thank goodness. She did seem to be tiring, however, when the meal was ended.

"Don't make plans for this afternoon, Sukey. Miss Lockharte will be resting."

"Nonsense, my lord. I am not at all tired. On the contrary, I am perfectly capable of going with Miss Alton on her errands."

"Nevertheless, you shall stay home resting. I am not about to have you tumbling down the stairs again."

"I did not tumble, my lord, I was—"

"Ill with the influenza, which might recur if you are not careful."

Susan's head was swiveling back and forth between the

two. Even Lady Stanford was taking note of her son's solicitude toward their new guest. "I think Miss Lockharte ought to know what's best for her, Stanford," she said.

"May I live to see the day," Wynn muttered so only Rosellen could hear.

She carefully folded the napkin from her lap and stood, so that he and the other gentlemen were forced to their feet also. "If you recall our visit to my uncle this morning, my lord, I am not in your employ. Nor am I a child who does not know her own limits. I shall rest when I am tired and not when you order me to. Is that clear? Now, with Lady Stanford's permission, I am going to fetch my bonnet so that your sister does not have to wait for me."

Susan applauded and the dowager called, "Brava, Miss Lockharte." Then she turned to her son. "I like this girl, Stanford. She's not nearly the mealymouthed chit she looks."

Unfortunately, Rosellen ruined her grand exit by stumbling over a wheel on the viscountess's Bath chair. Wynn caught her just before her head would have hit the corner of the mahogany table. The words on his lips were not at all suitable for his sister's ears, so he left the room and headed for the stairs, Miss Lockharte's insignificant, underfed weight once more in his arms.

Chapter Twenty

$\mathcal{R}$osellen felt like a grain of sand shouting at the desert. On the other hand, in his lordship's hands, she felt as secure as a sleeping child rocked by the breeze. But she was not a child. She was all too aware of Wynn's hard chest, his strong arms, the spicy male scent of him. No, she did not feel like a child at all, and as he stood over her, after he placed her on the violet-patterned bedspread, that breeze was more of a cyclone blowing through Rosellen's senses. This would never do, she told herself. Why, she didn't even like the man. It was gratitude alone that was making her heart beat faster. Wasn't it?

"Now rest, confound you." Wynn glared down at her, almost daring Rosellen to move off the bed.

Annoyed at herself for her totally inappropriate response to his simple caring, Rosellen snapped, "Confound yourself! Stop giving me orders, Stanford. I am neither incompetent nor invalidish."

"So you're recovered enough to attend the opera this evening?"

Rosellen had been to the opera once during her brief London sojourn. She'd adored it. She also knew that the evening would not end until long past her usual bedtime. She would fall asleep during *Figaro* if she did not have a nap. "Hmph," she conceded with an unladylike snort. "But you could consider a person's feelings when you start issuing commands."

Wynn crossed his arms over his chest so that he wouldn't be tempted to shake the infuriating female. "Miss Lockharte, I have done nothing for days but think of your welfare."

He was correct, of course, which made Rosellen even more cross. "I said feelings, not welfare."

"Forgive me for offending you once again, Miss Lockharte, for considering your health more important than your tender sensibilities. Perhaps I'll have a change of heart and consign you to perdition, where I'm sure Old Nick is anxious to smooth your ruffled feathers."

"I am being beastly, aren't I?"

"Mule-headed, viper-tongued, and hornet-tempered. Are those beasts enough?"

Rosellen was relieved to see that he was smiling. "And childishly immature, I suppose. But I have been a straw in the wind for so long, you know, barely permitted an opinion for myself, that it is hard to bend anymore."

"And I am so used to giving commands that it is hard for me to respect your need for independence, now that you have it."

"You are also somewhat arrogant," Rosellen reminded him as her eyes drifted closed.

Wynn reached over and softly touched her cheek. "Only somewhat? I knew you were growing to like me, Rosellen Lockharte."

While Rosellen rested, Wynn went about his errands. He called at Tripp Hayes's residence, only to find the place shuttered, the knocker off the door. If the fellow wasn't in London and he wasn't in Bognor Regis, where the deuce was he? Tully Hadfield's rooms were already let out to a new tenant, who had no knowledge of the rake's whereabouts. Wynn did better at the Albany, where one of the lads who stood around waiting to run errands or hold horses knew that the Heatherstone twins were out shopping.

"Argufying, they was, over who got to pick the hats and who got to pick the gloves. Then they was drawing cards over who got to drive. I never seen the like. It were better'n a two-headed calf."

A two-headed calf had more sense than Miss Lockharte's abductors, but Wynn set out to find them. A man—or men—did not go around kidnapping innocent females without being called to account. Rosellen had acquitted them of nefarious intent, but Wynn was not so sure. He was about to make certain that there would be no repetition of the bizarre holdup—and no mention of it in public, either, or else. He wasn't certain what the else might be, pistols or swords, but he was not going to let those two nodcocks destroy Miss Lockharte's chances for happiness.

A gentleman could have his gloves made anywhere, but he went to Locke for his hats, so Wynn tried there first. The Heatherstones stood out in the somber establishment like a pair of peacocks. With their red hair, yellow Cossack trousers, and spotted neckerchiefs instead of cravats, they were the Beau's bad dream. Wynn asked them to attend him at a coffeehouse, rather than be seen at his club with the twin Tulips or in public.

"Just the ticket," one of them said. "We was going to call this afternoon, as soon as we had new hats to wear. Wouldn't do to call on a lady with a bare head, don't you know." The other nodded vigorously. "Uh, Miss Lockharte *is* staying at Stanford House, ain't she?"

"Yes, with my mother." Wynn spoke loudly for any listening ears.

"That's all right and tight then. We was going to have to call you out if you put her somewhere shabby, wasn't we, Tom?"

They were going to challenge him? Wynn almost left them in the street, but he wanted some answers. Like what had happened to their old hats.

"Can't keep 'em on our heads, don't you know, when we don't forget 'em places. I swear they make 'em too big."

Wynn was positive that the dandy duo had had nothing to do with Old Humidor's hat. Miss Lockharte was another matter. In the farthest reaches of a smoke-filled coffeehouse, Wynn turned on his most forbidding demeanor, the one he saved for cardsharps, pimps, and mothers of debutantes. He demanded to know the Heatherstones' intentions toward his houseguest.

"We was hoping you had intentions, is what. Our intention is to join the army."

Heaven help Wellington now, the viscount thought. The war with Napoleon would drag on another ten years with these two on the British side.

The other Heatherstone was talking. Wynn could see that they hadn't come away from the encounter with his groom and driver untouched either. One had a bruise on his cheek. The other had a cut above his eye. He didn't know which twin was which, though, and did not care. "My goal is to see Miss Lockharte creditably established, with no blot on her reputation."

"Our goal, too! That's why we was hoping you'd come up to scratch."

Wynn pounded the table. "Once and for all, I have not dishonored the female and I am not going to marry her." He chose to ignore the times he'd been alone with her in various bedrooms, the urge he'd had just today to touch her cheek. He had no business wishing to see her eyes light up with laughter, and the Heatherstone twins had no business questioning his motives. "Do you understand?"

The Heatherstones understood that their heads would be pounded next. "Uh, does that mean one of us has to?"

Wynn could get rid of his new charge with one word. He could have her wed to one of these moonlings with a single nod. With Haverhill's dowry she could set up housekeeping, have little red-haired infants at her skirts. He shuddered at the thought. And what if the gossoon groom still wanted to join up? Rosellen might be a widow, which might be a blessing, or she might feel she had to follow the drum. No, she was altogether too delicate for that.

"You might ask her," he said, magnanimously allowing Rosellen a choice he knew she would not take, not if she wished a marriage of mutual affection and respect. "If it matters, Haverhill has agreed to dower the chit."

"I say, Tim, then you can marry her. The pater would approve."

"Deuce take it, I wanted to go to the Peninsula. Wellington don't take married blokes as aides-de-camp."

He didn't take morons either. Wynn had to smile, imagining Miss Lockharte's reaction to these two fribbles arguing over which one should ask for her hand. "Perhaps it won't come to that. I have hopes of introducing her to other eligible gentlemen, so she might have a choice."

Tim slapped his brother's shoulder with relief. "They always said he was a downy cove."

"No, he just don't want us to marry her, any more'n he'd want his sister to."

So there was a glimmer of intelligence in them after all, Wynn thought. "I have decided that, for the upset you have caused the lady, you will help my mother and sister bring her into fashion, steer her away from unsuitable matches, and otherwise keep your traps shut about her rather spotted past. Is that clear?"

The ice in his stare was clear enough. So was his aim, the Heatherstones knew. They gulped, their Adam's apples bobbing in unison, and nodded. Then they used their neckerchiefs to mop their foreheads when he left.

"High-handed sort, what?" Tom asked.

Tim agreed. "I don't think he'll do for our Miss Lockharte after all. Nasty temper, what?"

"And he gave the cat to that innkeeper. So what'll we do?"

"We know every chap who's on the lookout for a leg-shackle, so we introduce her around, make sure they know about her dowry, see if we can't get her riveted before we go off to Spain. That will satisfy our honor and satisfy Stanford. Meanwhile we can get her that dog she always wanted."

"But she's staying at Stanford's house."

"A big, ugly dog."

On his way home, Wynn stopped into Madame Celeste's and mentioned to that discreet modiste that a friend of his sister's was staying with them, Baron Haverhill's niece, to be exact, and the chit would need a new wardrobe. On the baron's tab, of course. Miss Lockharte would be in as soon as she was rested from her journey to Town and her recent illness, but could Madame begin a gown now, so she would have it to wear to her first ball? Wynn offered to pay extra, to give Susan's school friend a treat. The gown should be loose, so she did not look malnourished, and one sleeve must be cut wide enough to accommodate a splinted, plaster-wrapped wrist. Oh, and the gown had to be silk, and it had to be turquoise, the color of the Caribbean. Madame Celeste wrote down his instructions carefully, trying to hide her knowing grin. Miss Alton's little friend, eh? Celeste was a Frenchwoman. She knew better.

At Stanford House the ladies were taking tea. Wynn joined them as soon as he'd conversed with Stubbing and checked the post. His eyes went immediately to Rosellen when he entered the drawing room, to make sure she looked rested, he told himself. She did, with an attractive blush to her cheeks that he did not think came from the paint pot.

"My groom Roger has returned from Worthing," he told her while his mother and Hume discussed the day's politics and his sister was regaling Stubbing with the story of the opera they were to see that evening.

Rosellen leaned forward. "Did he find Fanny? Did he bring her back with him? What did she say about the money?"

Wynn smiled at her eagerness. The animation lent a sparkle of little golden flecks to her eyes. She'd do, he thought, when the ton got a good look at her. "He found your friend," he told her, sorry he did not have better news to keep her smiling, "but he did not get to speak with her. She is ill, at an aunt's house about ten miles outside of Worthing. That's why no one in the town knew her whereabouts."

"And she was too ill to speak to Roger? Oh, never say poor Fanny caught the influenza after everyone else recovered!"

"No, she developed a congestion of the lungs after taking a tumble into the stream on her way from the school. Her aunt is confident she will recover."

"She fell into the water?"

"According to the aunt, your Fanny did catch some of your, ah, imagination. The girl was babbling about someone pushing her. Who would try to harm a little maid on her way home from work?"

Rosellen thought a minute. "Was she wearing my red cloak?"

"I have no idea, but what you are suggesting is preposterous. The girl most likely did not want to be thought clumsy for slipping on the bank or some such. At any rate, she had no money on her when the family finally got her home. The aunt would have found it."

"I never expected Fanny to have the money. She is not a thief, I told you that. But will she be all right?"

"Yes, and Roger is to take back a message, telling her that I shall send a carriage for her as soon as she feels able to travel to London. I thought you might wish to have a familiar face around you, and she seems to be out of a position. Meanwhile, since there is nothing to be done about the, ah, missing purse, you can devote your energies to enjoying yourself for a change. Are you very disappointed?"

"That I can go to the opera and the museums and the park? Or that I shall have to apologize all over again, my lord, for thinking the worst of you?"

Chapter Twenty-one

*I*f ever a man existed who had every right to be puffed up with his own conceit, Rosellen thought, it was Wynn in evening clothes. She had never seen him dressed formally before, in a midnight coat and white satin knee breeches, and the sight quite took her appetite away, despite the dishes he kept pressing on her at the dinner table.

The viscount was magnificent from his wavy dark hair to the gold buckles on his shoes. Compared to his elegance, Rosellen felt like a milkmaid. She was wearing another of Susan's made-over gowns, this one an ivory satin with a blond lace overskirt, and knew she'd never been dressed better. She also knew she looked shabby and shopworn compared to her benefactor. Rosellen had begun referring to Wynn as such in her mind, for he was neither friend nor relative, employer nor guardian. Whereas she used to think of him as a sneering, self-important villain straight out of one of Mrs. Radcliffe's novels, the viscount had done her more good than anyone else in her recent past. And she still could not figure out why. She was nothing to him, and nothing compared to him or the women he usually associated with. The difference in their stations was as obvious as the difference between the diamond in his cravat and the circlet of rosebuds in her hair. Rosellen's thoughts tied knots in her stomach.

So bemused was she that, besides not doing justice to the sumptuous meal, she was not paying attention to the conversation around her. They were dining *en famille* again, since Rosellen, Stubbing, and Lord Hume were considered part of the household, it seemed. The older gentleman would stay on, keeping Lady Stanford company over a deck of cards, while the younger people attended the opera. They had been bickering good-naturedly about the stakes. Hume did not believe in taking substantial monies from females; Lady Stanford did not believe she would lose.

Rosellen stopped her woolgathering to listen when the viscount announced the receipt of a letter from Cousin Lenore and the solution to a mystery. She wished she could find the answers to her questions, too.

"Two solutions," Stubbing contradicted. "You've been wondering what became of Mr. Hayes."

Susan frowned at the thought of her unwanted suitor returning to the scene. "Nothing could happen to that old stick, Wynn, but when is Cousin Lenore coming back?"

"She's not, it seems. Cousin Lenore and that old stick, who incidentally is exactly my age, brat, have eloped to Gretna Green."

"Together?" Susan dropped her fork.

"That's the way elopements usually take place, Sukey."

"Why ever did they do a damn fool thing like that?" the dowager wanted to know. "Causing a scandal for no reason but to make themselves an item. It's an unexceptionable match and they are both adults; no one would have stopped them."

"Chits get romantical notions," Lord Hume reminded her, "even widows."

"There is nothing remotely amorous about a long, cold carriage drive to Scotland," Lady Stanford disagreed. "Flowers are amorous, and champagne toasts and organ music, not the sound of a hammer on the anvil in the background. I thought Lenore had more wits than that."

"I am afraid I am partially to blame, Mother," Wynn confessed. "I confided my hopes that Hayes would offer for Susan. Lenore feared she was being disloyal. Tripp knew my wishes also and did not want to embarrass Susan, in case she had expectations."

The dowager harrumphed. "So they go behind your back and carry on a secret courtship, the clunches. Now that is disloyal. I hope they enjoy the countryside, for neither will be accepted in London again."

Susan was laughing. "I still cannot believe it of your friend, Wynn. Weren't you always nattering on to me about what a steady, reliable fellow he was, how he would never be guilty of the least indiscretion? And he, your raft of rectitude, your pillar of propriety, just ran off to Scotland. With Cousin Lenore, my watchdog. Oh, dear, it's too, too delicious. I wonder if he carried her off over his saddlebow, or if he had to climb a ladder to help her escape? What do you think, Lieutenant Stubbing? What's the proper way to conduct an elopement?"

Wynn felt sorry for the scarlet-faced subaltern. "There is no proper form whatsoever and well you know it, so stubble it, brat. Will you stop laughing if I acknowledge that I was wrong?" Wynn turned to Rosellen, to include her in the conversation. "You see, Miss Lockharte, I am not infallible."

"I never suspected you were, Lord Stanford, but it is nice to see that you admit to being human."

"Have another portion of pheasant, Miss Lockharte."

"Isn't he divine?" Susan whispered in Rosellen's ear when they were settled in the first row of Wynn's opera box. Stubbing and the viscount were seated behind them. Rosellen glanced back. Yes, he was divine, much too godlike for a mere mortal. She was beginning to distrust her own all-too-human feelings. "I suppose he is passable."

"Only passable?" Susan was disappointed. "I think he looks

heavenly in his dress uniform. I wouldn't mind if the tailor never finishes his formal outfit."

"Oh, the lieutenant. Yes, he is very handsome." In truth, he could not hold a candle to the elegant nobleman beside him. Rosellen looked to see her friend's reaction to such tepid praise. She did not wish to encourage Susan in her matchmaking schemes, so she added, "If you like fair-haired gentlemen. I much prefer dark hair myself."

And half the other women in the vast horseshoe-shaped theater seemed to also. Rosellen saw nothing but the enormous chandeliers' lights reflected off quizzing glasses, opera glasses, and monocles, all aimed in their box's direction. Susan was getting her share of admiring glances, and Rosellen even supposed she was under scrutiny as a newcomer in the Stanford party, but almost every female eye that she could see was directed at Lord Stanford himself. The nearest females were waving their fans, bobbing their feathered headdresses, and casting sideward smiles, hoping to gain his attention. She would wager her newfound pin money that he didn't care what *those* highborn ladies had had for dinner. Her satisfaction was small, however. The viscount was obviously trying to fatten her up, like a pig for market, the quicker to get her off his hands in the marriage mart.

He was bound to be disappointed. Despite her uncle's sudden generosity—she supposed he wished to be shut of her also—Miss Lockharte was still a vicar's daughter with a dicey reputation. She wondered how long Susan's friendship would last when her companion was snubbed by the social world, how long Stanford's patience would hold out if no one offered for her. Rosellen could only hope that Fanny had recovered by then, so that she could retrieve her nest egg. Meanwhile, her confidence was cracked. She hardly noticed the singers onstage, worrying about the swells in their box seats.

At the first intermission, though, Stanford was proved correct once more. The box was overflowing with young men—and their hopeful sisters—come to meet Miss Alton's friend.

While some of the young ladies had been pupils at Miss Merrihew's and would have ignored a mere schoolteacher, they did not dare offend the most eligible gentleman in town. And the Heatherstone twins were there, too, introducing Rosellen to the patrons of the pit, voicing loud asides as to each young gentleman's qualifications and expectations.

"But how did you enjoy the opera?" Rosellen asked, to stop the embarrassing flow of names and incomes. "Did you find the soprano in good form tonight?"

"If the soprano is the one with the deuced loud caterwauling, I'll say she was in prime shape. Never seen a female with a bigger chest."

Susan giggled and Wynn scowled. The silent twin kicked the speaker.

"Well, stands to reason if she's to make that much noise, she'd need big—"

"Not in front of the ladies," his brother hissed.

"But Miss Lockharte is a regular right 'un. She didn't cut up stiff about the—"

A firm hand at the back of his neck was propelling the jackanapes out of the box. "Do not go into the diplomatic corps, if anyone is foolish enough to take you," Wynn muttered as he pushed the twin down the hall.

The other redhead followed, after promising to pay a call the next day with a surprise.

"Aren't they the drollest pair?" Susan asked. "I didn't know you knew the Heatherstones. I wonder what the surprise could be."

The surprise would be if they remembered their mission by morning, but Rosellen merely said, "Oh, yes, we are, ah, long-standing acquaintances." Then the lights dimmed again, thank goodness, so she did not have to answer any further questions.

Wynn was not happy with the way all the men were ogling Miss Lockharte. Granted, any female in his box would have come under review, but that she was known to the Heatherstones seemed to add to her attraction. And she was devilishly pretty, in a wispy, ethereal sort of way, with a ready smile and gentle courtesy. She didn't show the boredom affected by so many of Society's chits, and she didn't show the sharp edge of her tongue either, thank Heaven. Still, she wasn't used to such public scrutiny; she might be offended. Besides, she was not very strong yet. She should be home resting, not in the goldfish bowl of the *belle monde*.

At the next intermission, Wynn was going to suggest they leave before the hordes of bucks and bloods descended on the box, but Miss Lockharte sparkled. She was delighted with the opera and with her reception. He could no more drag her away than he could let the Heatherstones make her adventures public knowledge. Instead, he suggested they take a stroll in the halls, for some fresh air and perhaps a lemonade.

Wynn was careful to shield her broken wrist from any jostling, he was painstaking about draping her shawl over her shoulders, and he was mindful to herd his party away from gossipmongers and lorgnette-wielding matrons. Still, the color fled from her face and she would have stumbled but for his hand under her elbow. Wynn could feel her tremble.

"My cousin" was all she whispered.

"What, the indomitable Miss Lockharte fazed by a mere female, and a relative at that?" he teased, trying to ease her mind. "I thought you had more bottom, my dear, shooting up inn yards, herding off abductors, surviving rampaging draft horses. Clarice Haverhill is nothing but a toadstool, you know. She cannot eat you."

"No, but she can broadcast my disgrace and bring shame on you and your sister for introducing me to the ton. She hates me. Last time she succeeded in getting me tossed out of London in less than two weeks. This time she can—"

"She can go to the devil." Now Wynn was the one frowning. Didn't the chit have any confidence in him at all, in his power to protect her from one jealous cat? Hell, he'd been fending the creature off for ages.

"Miss Haverhill," he called. "Well met."

Clarice turned around to find the viscount bearing down on her, his party in tow. She looked to make sure everyone else in the crowded hallway noticed also. She stepped away from her own companions, the chicken-chested Duke of Rafton and his stiff-rumped mama. Now this was more the thing, Stanford wanting to exchange pleasantries with her. Clarice pasted on her best smile. "Lord Stanford, how delightful, and Miss Alton, too." She ignored Stubbing altogether. A lieutenant with a limp was beneath notice. Besides, he was known to be Stanford's secretary. "And Miss—"

Clarice screeched louder than the contralto on the stage. Her face took on an angry flush and her eyes narrowed to slits. "You!" she spat.

"Why, yes, it's your cousin, Miss Haverhill." Wynn stated the obvious with obvious pleasure. Her lily-livered father had evidently not informed the shrew of the treat in store, so it fell to him. "How kind of you and your family to lend us her charming company for the Season. My sister was pining for company of her own age to share the excitement, don't you know, so she begged Miss Lockharte to come to us. You must remember how it was when you were first out."

Clarice ignored the slurs to her age and the number of Seasons she had gone through. Stanford could not be squiring her cousin around! He simply could not. "But she's a schoolteacher! She's a hoyden! She's—"

"A guest in my home." Wynn spoke quietly. "I am sure you will be calling on us to see how she goes on." Which meant, of course, that if Clarice Haverhill ever wished to speak to the viscount again, she'd have to play the doting relative to her cousin. He turned his back on the fuming female. "Your Grace, may I make you known to my sister's friend, Miss Rosellen Lockharte? My mother quite dotes on the chit already, almost like another daughter."

The duchess looked from the clench-jawed, raven-haired harpy on her son's arm to the pale, delicate deb on Wynn's. Miss Lockharte was making a gallant curtsy, despite the cast on her wrist and the cousin's waspishness. Her Grace knew which she'd prefer for a daughter-in-law. "A favorite of Lady Stanford's, eh? I'll send round an invite to my next do. Come, Rafton, Miss Haverhill, we can miss the next act. This one's been interesting enough."

Chapter Twenty-two

*L*ife was full of surprises. For two years at the academy, Rosellen's days had been remarkably unchanging: the same gray gowns, the same apathetic students. Changing from upper-case letters to lowercase ones had been a big event, switching from chalkboard to pen and ink a major diversion. Since her illness, nothing was the same from one hour to the next, not her footing, not her feelings. The world was still spinning, and her brain was not even concussed.

Like when they returned from the opera to find Lady Stanford and Lord Hume playing three-handed whist with Wilkins, the butler, and all three were sipping brandy and smoking cigars. Was this how real ladies conducted themselves? The viscount had hurried her past the open parlor door, saying, "Don't even think about it. I try not to."

Like the drawing room filled with floral offerings the next morning, many of them for Rosellen. She could not remember the faces that went with half the cards, yet these gentlemen were sending her bouquets. One nosegay was from the Duke of Rafton. So what if his mother had pushed his graceless grace into doing the pretty? Rosellen Lockharte, disgraced penmanship instructor, of no particular face or fortune, was receiving flowers from a duke!

Like how annoyed Lord Stanford had been to see all the baskets and vases. He'd stormed off to his private office, looking thunderclouds, when he should have been delighted with her reception among the ton.

And like the dog. The Heatherstone twins arrived after luncheon, while the viscount was busy in his office with Stubbing, thank goodness. If Wynn hadn't liked the flowers, he was not going to appreciate the gentlemen gifting her with a dog, especially not this one. Rosellen could not imagine where the twins had found such a disreputable beast, but she was certain that the creature's owner had been happy to part with him. The animal was huge, for one thing. If the kitten was Noah, this mongrel was the Ark. Surely there were two of every type of insect residing in his mangy fur. He was also missing an eye, part of one ear, and most of his tail. And he snarled.

When Rosellen had thought of owning a dog, she'd pictured a fluffy little lap pet, a furry toy to cuddle and carry. She could almost ride this one. And he growled at her.

The twins assured her the dog was housebroken and friendly, once he got to know her. She noticed, however, that they left immediately after handing over the ogre's rope. Susan was no help, hiding behind the sofa.

"Nice doggie."

"Grrr."

"This isn't going to work."

"Toss him a macaroon," Susan suggested from her position of safety. "Dogs aren't supposed to bite the hand that feeds them."

No one had told the troll. Luckily his teeth slid harmlessly off the heavy bandage on her wrist. Susan said, "I think he wants another."

The enormous mutt ate all of the macaroons, an entire poppy-seed cake, the remaining contents of the teapot, the milk pitcher, the sugar bowl, and two napkins. Then he lay down on Rosellen's foot and went to sleep. She took a step backward and he growled.

Rosellen decided that she did not really like surprises. There was something to be said, after all, for monotony.

Uncle would turn purple with apoplexy at the price of Rosellen's ball gown. Aunt Haverhill would go ashen at the low cut. Clarice would turn green with envy. Rosellen was pink with pleasure.

In her aquamarine silk gown, Rosellen felt pretty for the first time in her life, especially when the viscount smiled appreciatively. Why she should care about his approval was beyond her; the man had all but ignored her existence during the past week, hidden away in his office, except for reminding her to dress warmly, get adequate rest, and eat all her vegetables.

Wynn did look devastatingly handsome tonight, though, and was flatteringly attentive at her first ball since coming to London for the second time. After seeing her and his sister through Lady Rafton's receiving line, he guided them to gilt chairs along the side of the ballroom, where Susan, guarded by Stubbing, was instantly surrounded by her admirers. The viscount asked Rosellen for the first waltz and held her carefully, solicitous of her wrapped wrist. Then he made sure she was comfortable, with the Heatherstone brothers and some of her other new friends to keep her company while she sat out the more sprightly dances, since her injured wrist would never withstand the twists and turns of the vigorous country sets. Only then did Wynn leave her to perform his own duty dances.

The light went out of the ballroom, it seemed to Rosellen. Her excitement at being part of the polite world evaporated. The people were dull, the music too loud, the perfumes too strong. Making polite conversation with gentlemen during the quadrilles and landlers and Sir Roger de Coverleys was worse than having to dance with them. How many times could she discuss the weather, her visit to the Royal Academy to see the artwork, or the king's health? And how many times could she watch the viscount dance by with some diamond-bedecked beauty on his arm?

She was being a peagoose, Rosellen told herself, turning her attention to Tom and Tim Heatherstone, who were babbling about a duck race. Then Clarice was there, telling the boys that Colonel Throckmorton was in the card room, talking about his regiment. Did they wish her to introduce them? Clarice had called at Stanford House once, found the viscount absent, and departed with the barest of courtesies to Rosellen, which suited both cousins. Now she was relieving her of the Heatherstones, most likely thinking to steal Rosellen's beaux. Clarice would never go off with both brothers if she knew how relieved her cousin was at their defection.

Unfortunately, Rosellen now felt conspicuous, sitting all alone in the crowded ballroom. In a way this was worse than when she was a wallflower at her own come-out, for then everyone had ignored her. No one had noticed whether the poor relation had had a partner or not. Now Rosellen could feel the eyes on her, judging, criticizing, pitying. There was that plain Miss Lockharte, she could imagine the tabbies saying, putting on airs above her station, and look where it's gotten her. She wished the dowager had come tonight, so that she could seek shelter under her chaperonage, but Lady Stanford was at home with Buck, the dog.

The dog did not growl at Rosellen anymore, as long as he was fed. She'd named him Buck, short for Buccaneer, for his missing eye and surly temperament. Nothing but a Barbary Coast pirate could be so mean. The stable crew vowed to hand in their resignations if forced to give him another bath, and the kitchen staff took to arming themselves with pots and pans, to defend the roasts and racks of baked goods. Buck did like a good meal, even if it was the viscount's.

He did like Rosellen in his way, too, his way being to sleep across her door or her foot or her lap when he could, lest she go anywhere without him, like to the kitchens or the park.

When she was not available for some reason, he adopted the dowager. Lady Stanford was delighted. She held on to his collar and Buck towed her Bath chair, so she did not have to call for a footman every time she wished to move. Usually he pulled her in the direction of the nearest candy dish or tea tray, but they were coming to terms.

Buck and the viscount were not. They mutually loathed each other, but Buck had quickly learned that he'd be sent to Coventry for showing his teeth to their host. Rosellen offered to get rid of the dog, if she could find him a good home.

"What, one with no children, small pets, or strawberry tarts?" he groused, his favorite treats having disappeared down Buck's insatiable maw.

"Then I shall send him back to wherever he came from," she proposed.

"Hell doesn't accept returns," was all Wynn said before locking himself in his workroom. So Buck stayed on as part of the family. Rosellen wished he were there now. His conversation was more intelligent than the Heatherstones'.

Thinking of Buck made her hungry, so Rosellen decided to find the refreshment room. She'd be less obviously alone there, and might find a potted fern to sit behind or something.

There were no tall plants, but Rosellen did take her cup of punch to stand next to the drapery by the French doors to the balcony, where she was away from the stifling heat of the overcrowded rooms. Her Grace did not believe in letting in the night air, so one door was open a bare crack. She did not believe in encouraging young people to get up to hanky-panky by lanternlight, either, so the balcony was in pitch darkness. Rosellen was happy, thinking she might be less noticeable in the shadows.

Then, from behind, a hand grabbed her arm above the elbow. She looked around, a scream on her lips, but another hand was clamped over her mouth and she was being hauled out the doors, onto the balcony. In the dark, with the music echoing in her ears, Rosellen felt herself being dragged toward the edge of the balcony, until the metal railing was pressing into her.

"Now jump, blast you."

The orchestra was starting another waltz and Wynn was looking for Miss Lockharte. Where had the plaguey chit gone off to now? He'd had a miserable evening of it, watching her chat with one man after another, heads pressed close to be heard over the music. He was glad she was popular, he told himself, but deuce take it, he did not like the way those cads were looking down the narrow top of her gown. He should have had Madame Celeste add a lace fichu. He was responsible for the female, by George. Someone had to look after her. At home he let the dog do it.

Confound it, he thought again, he should have been the one to give her a dog, a proper dog, not the ravening beast the Heatherstones had found for her. At least the creature earned his considerable keep by keeping the scores of gentleman callers in line. While Buck was on duty, Wynn knew none of the mooncalves would dare step beyond the pale, so he felt free to spend time in his workroom. Painting was not as relaxing as he'd used to find it, though, despite knowing his mother, sister, and Stubbing were nearby to protect Miss Lockharte from unwanted advances, if the mammoth mutt fell asleep on the job.

Who knew what could happen to her away from the crowded ballroom, though, if the chit went off by herself? She had as much town bronze as a baby bird. Wynn knew he couldn't sit in her pocket all night either, without stirring up a hornet's nest of conjecture. So he'd partnered his sister and two simpering debs, one dashing widow, and a friend's wife, who was all too willing to set up an assignation on the balcony. Wynn had made his escape, claiming he was promised for the next set, a waltz. Now all he had to do was find his partner.

He caught a glimpse of turquoise disappearing through the doors to that same suitable-for-seduction balcony and cursed under his breath. This time he'd strangle her for sure. He stormed over to the doors and wrenched them open, looking both ways to see where she'd gone. He spotted a man disappearing into the far shadows, his white neckcloth giving him away. He could hear Rosellen's heavy breathing nearby, damn it.

"By all that's holy, don't you know better than to come out on a deserted balcony in the middle of a ball? Are you trying to prove your cousin right? Didn't you learn anything?"

Rosellen tried to speak, but he was shaking her too hard. "He tried to . . . to . . ."

"I know what he tried to do, blast him; it's what every man in the room has been wanting to do all night!" Dash it, why should some bounder get to kiss the minx when Wynn was careful not even to think of such a thing?

"If you care so little for your reputation and mine," he said in a harsh whisper, "I might as well share the bounty, too." He pulled her closer, until her body was pressed against his hard chest, and then he lowered his lips to hers.

Rosellen was staggered by the weight of his anger, the accusations, the fact that he was actually kissing her. She could not have stood on her own without his firm support if her life depended on him, which it did, of course, but he wasn't giving her the chance to tell him. Oh, my, she thought, before she stopped thinking altogether, this was nothing like her first kiss, two years ago. This one might even be worth getting ruined over. She kissed him back, with all her inexperienced but awakening passion, just to make certain.

She was certain. And Rosellen was equally sure the viscount was kissing her only out of anger that she'd caused him more annoyance. He didn't like her, didn't respect her, and never believed a word she said, the worm. So she hauled back her broken right wrist and cracked him along the jaw with her new plaster cast.

Chapter Twenty-three

*W*hy did they call them the weaker sex? Wynn asked himself. This one could flatten him with a word, a look, a broken wrist. She could twist his words, twist his insides so he didn't know which way to turn. He turned to his workroom and his soldiers. They never answered back, demanded apologies for the unforgivable, or incited him to lunacy. Miss Lockharte did all three.

Why did she bother to speak, Rosellen wondered, when Wynn refused to listen? If his mother wasn't threatening to have a spasm over his behavior, he'd never come out of his office at all. She couldn't blame him for not wanting to show his contused cheek, but how was she to make him understand the danger?

She finally cornered him two days after the Rafton fete, stationing Buck at the morning room door so that the viscount could not escape into his private office after breakfast. She might have saved herself the effort. And the platter of sweet rolls.

"No, Miss Lockharte, I shall not listen to any more of this rumgumption. Once and for all, no one is trying to murder you. Reverend Merrihew would not even be in London, much less try to do you in, so that's just an aberration of your fertile imagination. Or perhaps some choice spirit poured Blue Ruin into the punch at Rafton's. As for the events on Rafton's balcony, the less said, the sooner forgotten. I have already apologized for my behavior, and I have given over expecting your apology for being out there in the first place. You must have learned by now that females who go off alone in dark corners must expect to be accosted. I was wrong, you were wrong. Drop it."

"It is not safe for me here, I say! What if Buck hadn't tugged so hard on his leash yesterday morning to get to that neighbor's cat? Both Susan and I would have been crushed by the roofing tile."

"Chimney caps and roof tiles fall off all the time in London, dash it. There was a wind abroad yesterday, not a woman-killer. You simply have to understand that not every mishap in the world is directed at you personally."

Rosellen was pacing. Buck's one eye was flicking from her to the viscount. "I'll remove to my uncle's. That way, if anything evil occurs, Clarice will be the one to suffer, not your family."

"What, do you think that Diamond will go walking your dog with you? Clarice Haverhill wouldn't be seen dead with a mangy creature like Buck." Or Rosellen, for that matter, but he didn't have to say it.

Hearing his name, Buck sat up, which put his nose at the level of the table, so he helped himself to the leftover kippers.

Wynn pointed at the disappearing herring. "Do you honestly believe your aunt will let that disaster of the dog world cross her door? Has she recovered from her visit here yet?"

"Buck did not understand about Aunt Beatrice's fur tippet." It was a feeble excuse, and Rosellen knew it. Worse, she knew Wynn was right: she could not take Buck to the Haverhills'. She didn't think there would be many rooming houses willing to take her and the problematic pooch either, even if she could get Wynn to advance her the fifty pounds.

He wasn't finished. "And what about Susan, if you leave? Did you think of how she would feel? She's never been so happy or so agreeable as since you came."

Rosellen had her own thoughts on that issue, too. She knew Wynn wouldn't want to hear them either.

"And my mother. She's introduced you to her friends, got you vouchers for Almack's under her sponsorship, and taken you into her heart. Why, that poor organ was so overwrought by the uproar at Rafton's that Mother has taken to her bed."

The viscountess had taken Miss Austen's new novel to bed, but Rosellen knew her son was determined to see things his own way as usual. Still, how could she leave them all? So she stayed, thinking it would serve the pompous peer right if she were slain on his doorstep. Then he'd have to keep Buck himself. But she never went out without a maid and a footman or Buck and his feral manners. She tried to keep Susan at a distance, and Stubbing and his loaded pistol in sight. Rosellen spent her waking hours looking over her shoulder, and her sleeping hours, what few she had, behind locked doors and windows, with the fireplace poker in her hand. The dark shadows were returning to her eyes, the pinched look to her mouth. Her temper was suffering as well as her looks. All of her pleasure in the visit was gone.

In the days that followed, Rosellen did not bother to mention the rock tossed at her horse in the park or the box of bonbons that arrived without a note. She'd set them aside for later; any creature without Buck's iron-clad stomach would have expired.

She thought of going to her uncle about the situation, but he had not believed her two years ago about a simple matter like a kiss. He certainly would not believe her story of a killer in clerical garb. Besides, the baron liked Miss Merrihew. He'd sent his sister's only child to the woman. No, she'd find no help there.

Stubbing was too busy with his lordship's correspondence

and his lordship's sister. The lieutenant assured her that the viscount was looking into the Merrihews' backgrounds, though, and he would tell her if the investigators found anything suspicious. A handful of attempts on her life did not appear to be suspicious enough, Rosellen thought angrily.

Bow Street was still a possibility, except that the viscount and Stubbing were right: she had no evidence. Buck hadn't left a crumb of a bonbon for her to have analyzed. Even if Fanny came to Town, swearing on her Bible that money had been delivered to the academy for Rosellen, the officials might not believe a poor maidservant. Justice, like dreams, was for the well-off and the well born, not for the likes of a Miss Lockharte or a serving girl who could not read.

Rosellen did write to Lady Comfrey, who had been Vivian Baldour. The former pupil at Miss Merrihew's was the only other person with fifty pounds whom Rosellen might have written to in her delirium. She'd heard since coming to London that Lady Comfrey had given birth to a healthy son, and that she and her elderly earl were in alt over the blessed event, in Bath. Rosellen congratulated them, wording her letter carefully in case Vivian was not her unknown patron. She wrote laboriously, using her left hand to support her right wrist, but she produced a clear, if obscure, letter. If Lady Comfrey wrote back, acknowledging Rosellen's gratitude, then she would have the beginnings of a case against the malfeasant Merrihews. And Lord Vance, too, for surely that had been Miss Merrihew's paramour holding up the coach. Mr. Merrihew did not ride as well and was of a less sturdy build. If she couldn't charge them with attempted murder, Rosellen decided, then thievery was a start. The authorities, and Lord Stanford, would have to take her seriously then. She'd never mention that the reverend was also a debaucher of young women, for that would be betraying Vivian, who was always a decent sort of girl, except for her scandalous association with Mr. Merrihew, of course, which was no one's concern.

Rosellen scratched on the door of Wynn's office and handed

the letter to Stubbing to post, noticing that the inner door was closed as usual. Then she went outside to join the ladies in Stanford House's rear walled gardens, where Lady Stanford was embroidering in the shade of the lilacs while Susan read aloud from the latest novel and Buck chewed on the leg of a wooden bench.

Not ten minutes later Rosellen was back inside and in Wynn's office. She did not bother to knock and she did not stop at Stubbing's desk. She shoved a sobbing Susan into the lieutenant's arms and marched straight through to the viscount's inner sanctum. Barely noticing that he was hunched over a worktable, wearing magnifying glasses and holding a paintbrush, she slammed a plain-hilted silver dagger down next to his elbow. "There," she shouted. "Is this evidence enough?"

"Bloody hell." Wynn's hand jerked, leaving a trail of paint across his sleeve. "Damn it, woman, I— Is that a knife?"

Rosellen was peering over his shoulder. She'd known he painted, of course, from the turpentine smell and the gossip. His avocation was one of the worst-kept secrets in polite society. "You paint model soldiers?" They were the most intricate miniatures she'd ever seen, and his brush was as thin as an eyelash. "They are exquisite."

Wynn had removed his spectacles to examine the knife. Although privately he was gratified by her evident appreciation, he was outwardly annoyed at the intrusion. "Confound it, Rose, you didn't barge in here to discuss my painting." Now he could hear his sister wailing from the other room. "What the deuce is going on?"

Also restored to her priorities by the other girl's cries, Rosellen shouted back, "That's what I'd like to know. This"—she pointed toward the knife—"was thrown over the fence at me, in your very own garden. If I hadn't bent over to take splinters out of Buck's mouth, I would have been skewered to a lilac bush. It missed your mother's chair by inches."

Wynn jumped up, knocking over his seat and two bottles of

paint. Rosellen rescued two unfinished soldiers from the spreading puddle.

"Your mother is unharmed. Wilkins and the footmen carried her upstairs. Her woman is with her, and the housekeeper, and her doctor has been called for, just in case. Susan is merely frightened," she added, when the viscount would have rushed into the outer office. "Stubbing is seeing to her."

Wynn was staring at the knife in his hand as if it had just bitten him. "My word, someone really was trying to murder you!"

"Is trying, Stanford. Is still trying! I told you and told you!"

"You also told me you were dying, confound it. You were out of your mind from the fever. How could I know what to believe?"

"I was dying, I just didn't finish. And someone—lots of someones, I fear—is trying to get rid of me, and he is not finished either."

"Oh, God, you could have been killed!"

"That's what I've been trying to tell you, you insufferable ass, but you would not listen. I was merely a hysterical female, so you wouldn't go to the magistrate or the Runners. You didn't even care about my fifty pounds." Rosellen put the miniature soldiers down carefully, lest she throw them at his head or drop them, her hands were shaking so from anger and fear.

Rosellen needed a handkerchief, but Wynn handed her a paint-soaked rag instead, with hands that were none too steady either. He managed a weak smile while he fumbled in his pockets for a clean linen. "You could have been killed," he repeated.

Then Rosellen was in his embrace, pressed as close to his chest as Wynn's strong arms could hold her. She could hear the furious pounding of his heart against her cheek. He was rocking, rubbing his chin on the top of her head, murmuring, "My God, I could have lost you." He held her tighter, as if he would never let her go.

Rosellen wept tears of relief. Here, she was safe and warm,

knowing he would protect her. Here was where she wanted to be, had always wanted to be, it seemed, despite knowing the lunacy of the pipe dreams she barely admitted to having. She raised her head for his kiss, and he obliged, as eager for the shared breath, the shared intimacy, as she. He would have surrounded her, filled her, blanketed her with his very being, if possible. That was what he told her in his kiss. He believed her; he believed in her.

Rosellen believed she'd finally reached Paradise. She had no awareness of her own body except where it touched his, no conscious thought except of him.

Wynn pulled back eventually, a question in his eyes, ready to duck her plastered arm. "It was worth it," he said. "And I won't apologize."

Rosellen knew what he was thinking, how wrong this was, how totally and abysmally unsuitable they were for each other in the eyes of the world. She was not sorry either. Even if there were no more moments like this one, it was enough. Her copy book was already blotted just by wanting him so badly, so Rosellen leaned into him again, finding his lips with hers this time. He did not push her away until another minute would have found them tumbled to the floor, with the door and various buttons open.

Wynn took a minute to catch his breath, tenderly combing her tousled curls with his fingers, paint stains and all. Then he said, "You mean there really was a stolen purse, too?"

Chapter Twenty-four

The Merrihews were missing. The academy was closed; the students were sent home early for the long vacation. The parents were told the hasty dismissal was to sanitize the building against another influenza epidemic. They were also told they had to pay next year's tuition in advance, to help pay for the disinfection. Miss Merrihew, it was given out, was taking a walking tour in Scotland, where her brother was supposedly at a theological seminary. If so, it was for the first time, since, according to the report Stubbing finally received, there were no records that the man had ever been ordained. There were no records that the man and his sister had ever existed until fourteen years ago, when they had used aliases and forged references to establish the school for daughters of wealthy families. Now the archbishop was sending his own investigators to see if Merrihew had performed any weddings as fraudulent as the education the young ladies had received.

Someone had warned them, most likely the same someone who had told Merrihew where to find Rosellen Lockharte. Clarice admitted to seeing the gentleman in London during the past fortnight, when he'd called to ascertain Rosellen's well-being. Naturally she had given him her cousin's direction. Hadn't he stopped at Stanford House? And no, Clarice had no idea where he was staying.

Wynn posted guards. Then he hired Runners to watch the guards. And called in Stubbing's army friends to watch the Runners. The ladies at Stanford House were better protected than any sultan's harem. Rosellen especially was not permitted outside the house, not even to the garden, without a battalion of watchdogs, besides Buck.

By unspoken consent, she and Wynn would not speak of what had happened in his workroom until the danger was past, if then. Rosellen knew nothing could come of it and did not want to hear him tell her so. She also knew without being told that Wynn did not want his model painting to be bruited about. She could have looked at the detailed miniatures for hours, but he had firmly locked the studio door behind them, effectively shutting her out of another part of his life. Yet he could not have done more to protect her.

Perhaps he was doing too much. "Merrihew will not attempt anything with all your men about," she complained. "So they'll never catch him."

"I've been thinking the same thing. The situation is intolerable, never knowing where he is or if he'll ever show up again. I've been considering hiring an actress to dress up as you to draw him out of his lair."

"What, and endanger another poor girl?"

"So what do you suggest, we stake you out like a lamb for slaughter? You are not leaving this house without my company and that is final."

"So I am a prisoner here?"

"Don't be getting dramatic on me, Rosellen. I am—"

"I know, only acting in my best interests. What about Vauxhall?"

"What about it? Surely you don't think we'll be attending the pleasure gardens this week with an assassin on the prowl. With all its dark paths and isolated grottoes, we'd never be able to guarantee your safety."

"But it sounds like the perfect place to set a trap. You and your men could be hiding in those dark places, waiting for him to approach me."

"Unless he uses a rifle this time. You could be in his sights long before we have the dastard in ours. Even a pistol gives him the advantage of not having to come so close. It is much too dangerous, kitten. You've used up enough of your nine lives."

"I do not think he'll suddenly use a pistol, though, when he hasn't ever before. A gun is too loud and too messy for the niminy-piminy fellow. I think my going to Vauxhall is an excellent plan."

"No, and don't argue."

"You promised you'd take me to see the fireworks."

"They will be there after we capture Merrihew."

But Rosellen might not be. She couldn't bear for Wynn to start treating her like another recalcitrant little sister again. She'd go back to her uncle's, where her heart wouldn't shatter a little more every time she saw him.

First she would go to Vauxhall.

Escaping from Stanford House was pitifully easy. Rosellen would have to inform the viscount that he was not getting his money's worth from the guards he'd hired. Of course, she acknowledged, they were stationed around the perimeter of the house to watch for anyone going in, not for someone coming out. Especially not a maid in a dreary gray gown and drooping mobcap going out to walk the dog. Rosellen's old uniform was shapeless enough that a pretty pink frock fit right under it. No one noticed her at all, in their efforts to give Buck a wide berth.

She told the family that she was going to bed early and no one wondered, with all the upset. With a disgusted look for her son, Lady Stanford noted that she herself would never have made it through the trying week without her dear Theo's comforting presence. Susan nodded, clutching Stubbing's arm.

Rosellen told the staff that she did not want to be disturbed until morning, and they were too well trained, and too nervous of the big dog who now shared her bedroom, to disobey.

She told Buck not to bark as she climbed down the back stairs and out the service entrance without seeing anyone.

Rosellen felt terribly guilty, lying to everybody who had been so kind to her. But she also felt guilty over making them captives in their own home and for placing them in danger, so she knew she was doing the right thing. And she did leave a laboriously written note for Wynn propped on her pillow. If she did not return, one of the maids would see that he got it in the morning.

Not a total gudgeon, Rosellen knew she could not handle Merrihew on her own, so she had made arrangements. Wynn wouldn't help, but the Heatherstone twins were ripe for the adventure, of course. They were waiting for her at the corner in a hired coach, pistols primed, hats pulled over their brows like desperate brigands—or boys playing at pirates. They had ropes and whistles and riding whips and a cricket bat. Duly impressed, Rosellen expressed her admiration for their foresight and enthusiasm, wondering to herself how her two redheaded white knights thought they would bring their arsenal into Baron Haverhill's private supper box. The pistols fit in their pockets, at least.

Chapter Twenty-five

*W*ynn was worried. He was also *de trop* in his own drawing room. Susan and Stubbing had their heads together at the pianoforte; his mother and Lord Hume were playing at cards at the other end of the room. Neither couple invited him to join them. Hell, neither couple acted as if he existed. But that wasn't what had him pacing from one end of the room to the other. No, as soon as this other mess was settled, he'd see his womenfolk settled. It was high time his mother and Hume formalized their long-standing understanding, making sure no scandal could be attached to their past. And if Susan wanted Stubbing, well, it was not the best of matches, but Wynn was beginning to understand that there were more important things than aligning noble families with notable fortunes. The lieutenant was a dreadful secretary but an honest man, and Wynn knew he could get the cub a decent posting to Vienna or a seat in the Commons. He'd do.

But what would Wynn do if he couldn't keep Rosellen safe? He'd brought the young woman to London to restore her health and to appease his own conscience. She was miserable there, in constant danger outside the house, her virtue in constant danger inside. He could not have left her in Brighton.

Now, it seemed, he could not leave her alone. Not only did the poor puss have to deal with a homicidal cleric but a lascivious host to boot. Never in his life had Viscount Stanford acted so boorishly, almost tumbling an innocent female on the floor of his studio, for Heaven's sake. Lud, the female had a knack for making him feel small! And he'd never apologized for the episode in his workroom either. Heaven only knew what Rosellen was thinking of his intentions. Hell, Wynn wasn't clear about his intentions himself. He knew only that the impossible Miss Lockharte had wormed her way beneath his skin, straight to the tenderest part of him that he hadn't known existed. Now he ached because she was unhappy.

She was a regular trouper, his wild Rose, none braver or more full of pluck, but the worry and uncertainty were draining even her indomitable spirit, he knew. Wynn had to talk to her, to reassure her. He had to explain his own unfamiliar feelings, too. Perhaps speaking them out loud would clarify the muddled emotions for him as well. Wynn hoped so, for his nerves were tied in half hitches.

The evening was still young and he wasn't the least tired, so Wynn decided to approach Rosellen, in the hope that they could both get a decent night's rest. Calling at a young lady's bedchamber was entirely unacceptable, but Hell, he reasoned, he'd already kissed the chit twice. A man could be hanged only once. Besides, they were not likely to be interrupted, not with his mother and sister so besotted with their own beaux.

If Rosellen was asleep, Wynn did not wish to disturb her, so he scratched lightly at her door, then pushed it open, shielding his candle with his hand. The sitting room was empty. "Rosellen? Miss Lockharte?" He went through to the bedroom. The covers were turned down, but no one had been in the bed. Then he saw the note propped on the pillow and his heart sank to his toes, which made sense, for his stomach was in his throat. The fool had gone off to find Merrihew herself; he knew it without having to read the message. And she'd gone to Vauxhall, which was no place for a lady at the best of times.

Hellfire and thunderation, he should not have trusted the chit to be reasonable, to wait for events to unfold. She never had before. Why had he supposed she'd start developing patience and prudence now? If ever there was a filly who needed a firm hand at the reins, it was the preposterous penmanship instructor.

Wynn held the folded page closer to his candle. As expected, the message was addressed to him, in none-too-steady letters. As if she'd known what his reaction would be to her disappearance, Rosellen had written: *My lord, In case something unfortunate happens, I want you to know that you are still overbearing and arrogant. And I love you.*

Something unfortunate would happen, all right. He'd find the chit and then keep her in chains for the rest of her life. Right after he wiped at the tear that threatened to fall on the letter. He finally understood Lord Hume's attachment to his hat and what it held. Wynn would never willingly part with this token of Rosellen's affections either. He might wish to cut the first sentence off and save the rest, but half-cocked was typical of his little love. Wynn refolded the note and placed it in his breast pocket, then he set about rousing the neighborhood with his shouted orders for men, horses, and pistols.

Hume had to stay behind to comfort the dowager, but a grim-faced Stubbing was at Wynn's side in a flash, buckling on his sword. Yes, he'd do. Then they were off, tearing through the streets of London as if the hounds of Hell were nipping at their heels. Or Buck.

Knowing that her aunt and uncle were attending the fete at Vauxhall had helped Rosellen decide on her course. In their presence, she would not damage her reputation further by traipsing around the pleasure gardens unchaperoned, so Lord Stanford might not be so furious with her. He might just strangle her, instead of boiling her in oil.

The Haverhill ménage would be at Vauxhall, she knew, because Clarice had boasted of her new gown, her new hairstyle, and her new beau, an émigré French count. The gown was shot silver, the coiffeur was shorn curls, and the suitor was just shy of sixty.

"Not alone with those two rattles, are you?" Baron Haverhill asked his niece when she appeared at his private box. He didn't know about the attempts on her life; he simply still had hopes for Stanford.

Rosellen gestured vaguely behind her. "The rest of the party wandered off down the Dark Walks. I had heard it was not entirely *convenable*, so I stayed behind, knowing I could stop with you until they returned."

"Quite right, not at all the thing for young chits to be going off in the night."

But Clarice made an unladylike sound. "When are you going to stop acting like a such a green goose, Rosellen? Everyone comes to Vauxhall for some harmless flirtation. Isn't that so, *monsieur*?" She tapped the count's arm with her chicken-skin fan.

The Frenchman seemed more interested in getting up a flirtation with Aunt Beatrice than Clarice, until he discovered that Rosellen could speak French adequately enough to converse intelligently.

The Heatherstones distracted a furious Clarice with the latest gossip, Uncle Townsend took a nap after a surfeit of shaved ham and arrack punch, and Lady Haverhill chatted with the ladies at the next table. Buck foraged below the raised box for scraps.

Rosellen was beginning to think her plans were for naught. Another twenty minutes of listening to the count's heavy-handed compliments, Clarice's biting comments on everyone who walked past, and her uncle's snores, and she might die of boredom, saving Merrihew the effort. Just when she was about to suggest to the twins that they should go find their own party, a message was delivered, surreptitiously dropped into Rosellen's lap by one of the waiters as he passed. While the count poured out more punch, Rosellen unfolded the note.

There are words that can be spoken only in private, she read. *Come to the Temple of Venus as soon as you can.* The note was signed: *Stanford.*

Now if there was anything Rosellen Lockharte knew, it was handwriting. She had seen enough of his lordship's these last days in his house to know that this was not Wynn's script. The style was his, terse and commanding, but the viscount's writing was bolder, less slanted. Besides, this paper was of poor quality and had no crest. Success!

She could have made an excuse about finding her companions, but Rosellen was not entirely comfortable with leaving the Heatherstones in charge of her rescue, especially since they would not give her one of their pistols, remembering how she had shot the blue bottle. There was someone else, though, someone who would be a perfect decoy, someone who would have crawled through broken glass for a private coze with Wynn. So Rosellen waited until no one was watching and slipped the note under Clarice's reticule, which was next to hers on the table.

In a short while, Clarice asked to be excused to visit the ladies' retiring room. "You might as well accompany me," she sniped at Rosellen while the count draped her domino over her shoulders. "Your hair is a mess."

Her cousin would abandon her at the rest room, Rosellen knew, but that suited her perfectly. She made her apologies to her aunt and the count, gestured to the Heatherstones, hoping they understood that they were to follow her, and left in her beautiful cousin's wake.

Sure enough, Clarice was not waiting for Rosellen outside the ladies' chamber, but Tim and Tom were, with Buck.

"Do you know the way to the Temple of Venus?" Rosellen asked.

They didn't, and the first people they asked were two scantily dressed women, who wanted only to accompany the twins down the dark paths. "And your skinny friend can come, too," they offered. "But not the dog."

The brothers were in high gig, but Rosellen was feeling remorse at having sent her own cousin into danger. What if Merrihew had another knife and threw it first, without looking carefully at his victim? But no, any number of ladies and ladybirds were wandering around. He would have to make sure before assaulting anyone. Still, she hurried the twins down the paths, wishing she had a domino herself, to avoid the rude stares and crude remarks.

As they neared the small pavilion hidden behind some trees, lit only by the moon and the stars, they could hear Clarice's shrill voice: "What do you mean, what am I doing here? What are *you* doing here? You're not Stanford! And take your hands off me, you toad. You've already crushed my dress."

"It's a good thing for you I didn't crush your skull!" Merrihew snarled, tossing aside the rock in his hand. "Damn, where is your cousin?"

"I am sick and tired of everyone wanting my wretched cousin, by Heaven. You and Stanford and Rafton and now *le comte* Mercineaux. Why, even the featherheaded Heatherstones prefer her company, and she is poor!"

"I say," Tim called. "That's no way to speak about your cousin."

Merrihew spun around. When he saw Rosellen, he bent for the rock again, but Tom had his pistol in his hand. Merrihew grabbed for Clarice, to use as a shield. She screamed.

"Shoot 'em both," Tim advised, but Rosellen cried, "No!"

No was the word Buck heard most often in life. Thinking his mistress was calling him, the huge dog came barreling through the bushes, knocking down Merrihew and his captive to get to her. Tim handed his pistol to Rosellen and leaped on the reverend. So did Tom, but he landed on Clarice instead, who hadn't stopped screaming yet. Buck jumped up on Rosellen to lick her face and the gun went off. The statue of Venus atop the columned pavilion was blown to smithereens, spewing white powder over them all. A trysting pair inside the

203

temple staggered out, half dressed and more than half cast-away. "Ghosts!" the female shrieked, adding to the din.

"Not yet" came the soft comment from Wynn Alton, Viscount Stanford, as he walked down the path, pistol in hand. "Not yet, but soon."

Chapter Twenty-six

$\mathcal{V}$auxhall was vast and Rosellen was one small woman, but she had been remarkably easy to find. Wynn had only to follow the sounds of mayhem. Screams, shots, panicked party-goers, a dog barking—the frail female was definitely in the vicinity. He rushed ahead of his footmen and hired guards, pushing fleeing revelers aside.

Darkness, plaster dust, bodies on the ground—what the devil was going on and which one was Rosellen? As soon as Wynn made his presence known, a hysterical woman threw herself against his chest and he feared for a moment that Rosellen had been wounded, but it was Clarice Haverhill, peculiarly enough. Wynn passed her, still screeching like a banshee, into Stubbing's unsuspecting arms and bellowed for lanterns.

Rosellen was the one on the ground with the smoking pistol. Of course. Wynn lifted her up and removed the weapon, keeping his own pistol aimed on the others until he was sure who was who or what. He did not release Rosellen, and she made no effort to leave the shelter of his arms. She had grown some in wisdom, Wynn noted, for she was letting Helter and Skelter describe their great adventure. He kept his arm across her thin shoulders, both to reassure himself of her safety and to make sure she did not flit off on some other ill-conceived and unacceptable scheme.

"Well, children." Wynn spoke with controlled fury. Rosellen should have let him slay her dragons. She should have been safe at home. "Now that you've got your villain, at great peril to your persons, I might unnecessarily add, what are you going to do with him?"

The Heatherstones were not long on subtlety or sarcasm. Tim was sitting on Merrihew's chest, Tom on his knees. "Dash it, I knew we should have brought the rope," Tim complained. "We could string him up and save the Crown the cost of a trial."

The notion had definite appeal, but Wynn had to veto it. "Then you'd all be charged with murder, you nodcock."

"Shall I send for the constables, sir?" Stubbing wanted to know. "Or some of the lads and I could drive the dirty dish to Bow Street." He'd do anything to get rid of the clinging Clarice, who was still screaming in his ear.

"I have hopes of settling this a bit more quietly, to protect Miss Lockharte's privacy. She would have to testify, you know, which cannot be a comfortable thing. What say you, Merrihew, do you prefer to chance your fate with the courts? I suppose you might face transportation instead of hanging. Or will you take an offer of a passage to India? I know of a ship leaving this week, and I have enough contacts there to ensure your cooperation. Of course I'd have your signed confession before you left, guaranteeing that you'll never return."

"Confess?" Merrihew mumbled through cut lips and loosened teeth. "You cannot prove anything. I committed no crime."

Rosellen started to protest, but Wynn squeezed her. "You did not manage to succeed in your crime, rather, due only to your ineptitude. We can, however, prove that you misrepresented your credentials. I should think that those couples whom you married, who now find themselves living in sin, their children bastards, will have a few words to say at your trial. And there is the matter of Miss Lockharte's missing money."

"I never touched her blunt," Merrihew insisted. "That was Mirabel. I told her to let it go till the chit was dead, but she wouldn't listen."

"Ah, honor among thieves. Unfortunately, your sister seems to have flown the coop. You're the only one we can charge for all the crimes."

"Go to Hell. You have no evidence but the testimony of an attics-to-let antidote."

Wynn's arm tightened around Rosellen, while his fingers tightened on the trigger of his pistol. "You know, I believe I might have a better idea. The press-gangs are always out working the docks. . . ."

He did not need to finish. Merrihew whined, "I heard there are still opportunities in India."

"I regret inflicting you on the British populace there, but it does seem the most desirable solution. Do you agree, Miss Lockharte?"

Rosellen was about to give her opinion, now that Wynn had settled everything to his satisfaction, when she was pushed aside. Clarice took her place in his arms, sobbing into his waistcoat. "What about me, Stanford? I've been ruined. Just look at me, and all on account of your note to meet you here!"

Her dress was gaping at the bosom, and her hair looked like a squirrel had made a nest in it, but Wynn was not buying her tale. "I never wrote the note, as you very well know, Miss Haverhill," he said.

"How was I to know that? I came in good faith, and now my reputation is destroyed. You'll have to make things right, Stanford."

"Gammon," he said, trying to extricate himself from her barnaclelike embrace. "No one has to know you weren't with your cousin the whole time."

"What, a harum-scarum female of no account to anyone?

No one will believe her, and I'll be tarred with the same brush."

Rosellen was sputtering in the background, one hand on Buck's head to keep him from eating the lady's stocking he'd found on the pavilion's floor.

"Devil a bit," Wynn replied, free from her at last. "No one will doubt the credibility of the next Viscountess Stanford."

"Viscountess Stanford? That hoyden?" Clarice shrieked, while Rosellen had to hold on to Buck to keep from falling again. "You're going to marry me!"

"When Hell freezes over, madam. But there is always him." Wynn nudged Merrihew with his foot.

"What, I should marry a nobody like him? Never."

Wynn shrugged. "It's the best offer you're likely to get. You can live quite comfortably in India on your father's money, you know, and you might even become something of a social success there, daughter of a baron and all. Otherwise, of course, you'll be a pariah here. Once it is known how you conspired to ruin your own cousin, no one will recognize you."

Clarice looked to Stubbing, who instantly faded into the foliage. Then she stared from one Heatherstone twin to the other.

"We're joining the army," Tim informed her.

"Tomorrow," Tom added.

"The ship's captain can marry you on the journey over," Wynn prodded, anxious to end this contretemps. "Why don't you think on it overnight, discuss it with your father? Merrihew isn't going anywhere." He was going to the windowless basement of Stanford House, under guard, until Wynn could have him escorted to the India merchant ship. Of course Wynn promised himself a few minutes alone with the dastard first, but there was no reason to mention that to anyone. Perhaps Clarice would like her bridegroom better with his face rearranged. "I am sure the Heatherstones will escort you back to your box, unless, of course, they wish to stay and discuss with me how they happened to lead a young lady out of my house and into such peril."

The Heatherstone brothers each took one of Clarice's arms and towed her away, her sandaled feet barely touching the ground, they moved so quickly. Wynn gave orders for the disposal of Merrihew and the dispersal of his retainers. Only when they were all gone, including the spectators, did he turn to Rosellen. He placed his hands on her shoulders so that she faced him. Gently brushing the white dust from her hair, he said, "Without a doubt, Miss Lockharte, you are the most rash and reckless female I have ever known. What the devil am I going to do with you?"

"For a start," Rosellen answered, "you can kiss me."

He laughed. "Rash, reckless, and headstrong to a fault, and I do love you so, Rosellen." Then he bent to touch her lips with his.

This was better than any kiss that had gone before, Rosellen decided, because now he loved her. The ground trembled, the stars turned brilliant, the very air vibrated between them.

"Hmm," she said some minutes later, "I always knew I'd love fireworks, and they haven't even started yet."

Chapter Twenty-seven

"*I* take it that means yes?"

Rosellen opened her eyes. Wynn was inches away—miles too far—staring down at her. She licked her lips, savoring the taste of him. They hadn't moved farther than the bench in the ruined temple. "Hmm. What was the question?"

"The question was whether you were going to make me the happiest of men, but you already have. Now will you marry me?"

"Please don't tease, Wynn. I know you were only pretending for Clarice's sake, to get rid of her. I understand, truly, and you mustn't get any misguided notions of chivalry or such fustian. I was compromised long before I met you."

"Silly goose. I did not need an excuse for your cousin and I never pretend. You should know that."

"I also know that you cannot wish to marry me," she insisted.

"And I know that there is nothing on this earth that I wish more."

"But it would be a dreadful misalliance. We come from such different worlds."

"You *are* my world, Rosellen. That's all that matters. Besides, you do have a dowry, remember, not that I need it. And your birth is as good as my sister's, if not better, but that is a tale for another day. Your education is certainly better. And if your father did not have a title, so what? He had the wisdom and intelligence to raise a daughter with a mind of her own."

"You hate my independent thinking."

"Only when it collides with my viewpoint. Otherwise I think you brave and clever and loyal to your beliefs, everything I admire. But is it me you don't wish to wed, that you are making excuses? Are you afraid I'll ride roughshod over your feelings and opinions? You won't let me. Anytime I come the despot with you, you can sic your dog on me."

"You truly love me, despite my independent ways?"

"Do you remember the letter you wrote me?"

"Don't remind me of that idiocy, I beg of you!"

"But in it you spoke of all the things you never got to enjoy, all you'd miss if you were taken too early. You never had a dog, or a waltz, or a silk gown. I'd dress you in moonbeams and waltz you among the stars. Buck is another story, but you tore at my heart with your words about never holding an infant of your own. Rose, I cannot imagine greater joy than seeing you with my child, our child. I would give everything I own, everything I am, my prickly bramble Rose, just to see you happy."

"Oh, Wynn, you really mean it, truly?"

"Everything and then some."

They shared another kiss, after which Rosellen asked, "And fireworks?"

"I could never forget the fireworks, sweetheart. You said you never got to feel a lover's embrace. You will, as soon as I can arrange it."

"Never say I wrote such a thing!"

"I'm glad you waited, because I definitely wish to share that with you forever. But I was missing something, too. I thought I'd never know love, not if I lived to be a hundred and two."

"And now?"

"I was waiting for you, Rosellen. Only you."

Since she was still in his lap on the bench, it was an easy thing for Rosellen to throw her arms around Wynn and give him her answer. Sometime later, when Wynn felt her shiver, he pulled his caped greatcoat tighter around both of them. "We'll go to my Jamaican properties for our honeymoon. I have to see if your eyes really are the color of the Caribbean. Ah, if that's all right with you, my dear. Should you like to go there?"

"Anywhere with you, my love. Anywhere."

When the viscount and his lady returned from their bridal trip, a quantity of mail was waiting, with belated wedding gifts and notes of congratulations.

Rosellen looked up from her place at the desk adjoining Wynn's. "How strange."

"What's that, my love, that Stubbing left my correspondence in such a hobble? I daresay he was too busy making arrangements for Mother and Hume to go to Austria with himself and Susan. I only wish they'd taken the dog with them. The task of sorting through this mess would be easier if the blasted animal hadn't eaten half the letters."

"No, silly, this package. It's from Lord and Lady Comfrey, from Bath, I think. It seems to be a bank draft for fifty pounds, the last I'm to get, they write. At least I think that's what this part says."

"I should hope so. You won't be needing another wedding gift anytime in the foreseeable future, sweetheart. But I have an even stranger note." He held up an unwrapped parcel, bits of brown paper falling away to reveal two small metal soldiers, painstakingly painted in meticulous detail. "Tully Hadfield sends them from Wales, for the baby. I cannot make out if his guilty conscience was bothering him or he couldn't get a decent price at the fence's. It seems he just wanted to see my secret paintings, to find something to punt on tick. He found a wealthy mine owner's widow instead, and she has four—no, I think that's a five—girls, thank goodness, or he might have been tempted to keep the soldiers."

Rosellen touched her rounded stomach. "How did your friend know about the baby? And what if she's a girl?"

"Why, then, my darling Rose, we'll have to keep trying. Besides, haven't you been complaining about young females' educations and limited opportunities? What's wrong with my little aqua-eyed angel learning how to play with toy soldiers?"

Rosellen was piecing together yet another bit of mauled mail addressed to Lady Stanford. This one was written in pencil, in crude letters, with an even more disreputable page folded inside. The inner note was so old and worn, faded and blurred, that Buck's depredations had made it entirely unreadable. She could decipher the outer page, however: *Lady, I found this letter with your name on it. It were in a hat what was floating in a stream. Yer man must of loved you a lot. My donkey needed the hat.*

A widowed beauty . . . an aloof lord . . .
a scandalous past . . .
and a second chance at love in

HIS GRACE ENDURES

by Emma Jensen

When the widow Deirdre Macvail set out to accompany her sister-in-law to her first London Season, she never expected to encounter Lord Lucas Gower—the man she had quite literally jilted at the altar seven years ago. Deirdre is determined to avoid the grand, arrogant Lord Gower, but much to her astonishment, Lucas is the very picture of graciousness. In fact, he rescues Deirdre and her wayward charge on more than one occasion and is far more charming and agreeable than she ever remembered.

Could Deirdre have made a mistake in her first assessment of Lucas? Is there a chance for a great second love? Could "poor Deirdre of the Sorrows" become known at last as "Deirdre of the Dashed Good Fortune?"

Want to know a secret?
It's sexy, informative, fun, and FREE!!!

❦ PILLOW TALK ❦

Join Pillow Talk and get advance information and sneak peeks at the best in romance coming from Ballantine. All you have to do is fill out the information below!

♥ My top five favorite authors are: _____

_____

_____

_____

_____

♥ Number of books I buy per month: ❑ 0-2 ❑ 3-5 ❑ 6 or more

♥ Preference: ❑ Regency Romance ❑ Historical Romance
          ❑ Contemporary Romance ❑ Other

♥ I read books by new authors: ❑ frequently ❑ sometimes ❑ rarely

Please print clearly:
Name _____

Address_____

City/State/Zip_____

Don't forget to visit us at
www.randomhouse.com/BB/loveletters

metzger

**PLEASE SEND TO: PILLOW TALK/
BALLANTINE BOOKS, CN/9-2
201 EAST 50TH STREET
NEW YORK, NY 10022
OR FAX TO PILLOW TALK, 212/940-7539**